THE DIVIDED CITY

MARY E. TWOMEY

MARY E. TWOMEY, LLC

THE DIVIDED CITY

Book Three in the Last Deadblood Series

By

Mary E. Twomey

COPYRIGHT

Copyright © 2021 Mary E. Twomey LLC
Cover Art by Emcat Designs

All rights reserved.
First Edition: November 2021

This is a work of fiction. Any resemblance of characters to actual persons, living or dead, is purely coincidental. The author holds exclusive rights to this work. Unauthorized duplication is prohibited.

This book is licensed for your personal enjoyment only. If you would like to share this book with another person, please purchase an additional copy for each reader. Thank you for respecting the hard work of this author.

For information:
http://www.maryetwomey.com

DEDICATION

For Panda Bear

ABOUT THE DIVIDED CITY

Living in a city on the constant brink of war is about to cost Colette everything she holds dear.

When the vampires are tired of being tolerated instead of accepted, tensions between the two races begin to boil over. With her life at stake, Colette has to decide if staying in Mayfield is worth the toll it will take on her family, and her heart.

Escaping the violence of Mayfield seems to be the only option, but there is no telling if all she has fought for will be worth the sacrifice in the end. If the city cannot reclaim the best parts of itself, Colette is prepared to leave the city to its ruin, and turn her back on everyone she has fought to save.

"The Divided City" is filled with political intrigue and scandalous secrets, written by USA Today bestselling fantasy romance author, Mary E. Twomey.

TWO TANGLED HEARTS

COLETTE

*L*iving in Mayfield is a constant exercise in hurtling across new challenges while keeping your head aimed at your goal. While sometimes my goal is as pitiful as trying to make it through the day without my body betraying me and devolving into uncontrollable spasms, other times there are far more harrowing tasks added to my plate.

And one of those harrowing things is unpacking a box of my sweaters on the other side of my new house. It's been a long day of moving my things from my home in the East End—where my boyfriend could not cross territory lines to visit me—to a new place in Midtown down a dead-end street, where I have the only house on the road.

Even though Rome can go anywhere in Midtown, it would be the scandal of the century if it was found that a vampire and a human were dating.

So we keep our relationship quiet and the witnesses few.

How I wish I could shout our love from the rooftops.

Rome Valentino is the noblest, handsomest and bravest man I have ever known, and for some reason I still can't put my finger on, he has chosen me to read poetry to over the phone every night.

He is also a vampire, and I am a Deadblood. The Last Deadblood, in fact. My blood is the one weapon that can kill a vampire on the spot. Though I would never attack a vampire on my own, my blood has been stolen on many occasions throughout my twenty-five years to create weapons that might murder an entire race of people.

A people I love.

Aside from that obvious hiccup, the fact that I am a human and Rome Valentino is a vampire makes us an anomaly that people have never seen before.

And hopefully they never will. Keeping our relationship secret is the only way to keep it at all, in my opinion.

Plus, Rome isn't just a vampire, he is *the* vampire—the head of the Valentino family, who owns most of the property in the West End. He comes from old money and isn't afraid to negotiate with the powers that be (and often shouldn't be).

The fact that we are dating is something neither of our families would approve of, not to mention the rest of our respective people.

Despite the creeping worry about what would happen if my father found out about us, there is no part of me that is willing to push our relationship aside. I am hopelessly and madly in love with Rome, even if we are a clear danger to each other.

As I set down the box marked "living room crap" on the floor (thanks, Declan), the trepidation of the unknown zips through my veins. This house is new and unfamiliar, though I know that's no reason to draw a firm opinion. I want to like it here. Rome couldn't visit me in my old house, but here we have a chance at a normal relationship without so much red tape.

It's a nice house, to be sure. The walls have been freshly painted with sky blue in the living room, dandelion yellow in the kitchen, and of course lilac in the two bedrooms. The wooden doorframes, baseboards and wainscoting are bright white, framing the whole one-story home with a lightness that lifts my spirits, even as my back aches from moving about a million and a half boxes. The whole place looks like a feminine haven, and I love it.

Selecting the right home was an exercise in teamwork. I'd picked a two-story house closer to the West End. I wanted a two-story home because then I can challenge myself and prove that I don't need to live with someone. However, Rome and Declan both pointed out that being able to get to my bedroom on a bad day when my tremors call the shots is a blessing worth the cost of sacrificing the self-flagellating stairs.

Darn their solid logic.

When I moved back to my hometown after a decade spent living overseas, I did not anticipate packing back up and hauling my things fifteen miles west just to reopen them in Midtown.

Even though there is nothing odd about a human moving to Midtown, I still feel exposed. Our house is the only abode on this dirt road. I know Rome chose it for its privacy. It's a good thing. A smart move. However, I have no neighbors now, and the dirt road outside is devoid of any traffic.

We have to keep our relationship private. So far only my brother Declan knows and Rome's cousin, Orlando. I'm sure if either of them could shake us out of our syrupy affection for each other, they would.

If I could kick my infatuation with Rome, I would, but he is it for me.

I trot out to my car and take another box from the trunk, carrying it inside toward the bedroom, where Rome is unpacking my things. This box is lighter than the last one, thank goodness.

Even though this house doesn't feel like my home yet, I like seeing Rome in it.

Even as he hangs up my sweaters, I am enamored of his calculating movements. He has far more important things to do today than help me unpack. He even offered to send his men to do the job, but before I could answer, he'd shaken his head. "No. I don't want them in your space. I'll do it."

He hasn't tired, even though I have a great number of unnecessary items.

I pared down as much as I could.

"You're doing it again," he comments without turning his head toward me.

"What am I doing, exactly?"

"You're staring at me. Am I blowing your mind with the way I'm hanging your sweaters? What is it that has you so fascinated, tré-sur?" Then, just to make me laugh, he does a sultry sway, shaking his delicious backside as he shimmies down the closet door like a stripper who dances solely for me.

I love that only I get to see this side of him. The silly, sexy side of Rome is my joy. He's always serious and stoic with everyone else. I get to see his lips curving upwards and the laughter lightening his ice blue eyes. It's like his happiness is a present meant only for me to unwrap.

I move over to him when he rights himself, gluing my front to his spine so I can smooth my palm down his side and over his hip. I kiss the back of his shoulder and bury my face in his white undershirt. My free arm snakes around his taut abdomen. "Yes. It's the way you hang my sweaters. It's making you look absolutely irresistible."

"Remind me to tempt you with home organization more often. Mm." I love when he makes that contented, dreamy sound. Every time it vibrates past his closed lips, my heart swells.

I do that to him. *I* give him those moments of satisfaction.

I kiss the back of his shoulder once more. "I'm glad you're here, helping me with all of this."

"Are you kidding? You're the one who upended your life to move here. Unpacking is the least I can do. Plus, I want to know where everything is. If you're cold, I can't exactly go grab you a sweater if I don't know where they are."

It's the thoughtfulness that makes him so sexy, even more so than the nuances of his smile. Above his chiseled jaw, his thick black hair, leonine build and stunning features, it's his attention to detail that solidifies his place in my heart, and in my arms.

My hips are curvy while his waist is tapered. I love the distinctions that make our bodies move so beautifully together. He towers over my quaint five feet, yet somehow, we fit perfectly.

"I like the look of you in my home."

"Then I might not leave." It's the second hint he has given me that he would like to be a more permanent fixture here.

I don't know. I don't want him to see me unable to

screw off the cap of my meds. I don't want him to know that I sometimes have to take hot baths just to get my muscles to relax themselves. I know the whole point of me moving here was so he could help me if I needed it, but I don't want to need it. I really don't want that to be the reason we live together someday.

Footsteps coming down the hall remind me that we are not alone. Declan and Orlando have been helping us throughout the day. Declan's been moving the boxes while Orlando has busied himself installing the security system. "I just finished reinforcing the entrances," Orlando informs us as he enters the room. "Four keys—one for each of us."

My hands fall away from Rome, though not before I press another kiss to his body, this time in the center of his spine. I love when he shivers for me. He's so strong and steadfast. To undo his erect posture with a mere kiss?

I have never felt more powerful.

I cast Orlando a bright smile. "Thank you. You're my big sweetie pie. Did you know that?"

Orlando rolls his eyes at the doting only I can get away with. "I think I've heard you say that a few times. In public. Just to embarrass me."

"I say it because it's true." I lean up to press a kiss to his cheek—another thing only I get to do. Orlando has to lean down to accommodate my lack of height. He could keep his posture erect, but deep down, I know he likes the sweetness I bring to his life, or he wouldn't bend to it so often.

Orlando holds out his hand, showing me a small bag no larger than the size of my fist. "This is for you. Do you have a necklace it can go on?"

Rome rolls his eyes, exasperated that Orlando is flubbing up what is apparently supposed to be a precious moment. "You could have put it in a jewelry box. Made it more of a moment."

Orlando's upper lip curls in time with his eyebrow raising. "A moment for what? It's a necessity, not a romantic gift. You should be the one giving it to her."

Rome glowers at his beefier cousin. They look so alike, but for Orlando's bulkier build. "She won't take it if it's from me."

My head whips from one man to the other. "What are we talking about, here? What's in the bag?"

Orlando opens it for me and dumps the contents into my hand with no finesse.

Gotta love him.

My mouth pops open as I examine the small white gold charm. It's perfectly circular and about the diameter of a coin, though it's nearly half an inch thick. Engraved on the back are two hearts entangled in a way that makes them look incapable of pulling apart. There's a vertical line where the gold splits, running through the circle shape from top to bottom, but it doesn't separate the hearts.

"Wear it," Orlando commands, sounding like a caveman.

"Huh? You got me a charm? Thanks, Orlando."

My big sweetie pie rolls his eyes at me. "Obviously I didn't pick out something so… Rome got it but made me give it to you because apparently we're in middle school."

Rome shoves his cousin toward the door. "Well done. Out you go."

I tilt my head up at Rome, trying to keep up with their odd way of presenting a nice gesture. "Why didn't you want me to know this was from you?"

"Because you would forgive Orlando for being overbearing. It means something different if a boyfriend asks you to wear a tracker, rather than a head of security."

My shoulders lower. "Oh. This tells you were I'm at?"

"More than that. If you're abducted again, you just do this," Rome takes the charm from my palm and turns it sharply in half where the gold is split down the middle. Just like that, the two hearts are separated, the first on one side, and the second upside-down on the other side. Then he tugs out a chain from beneath his shirt. "I've got one, too. If you do that, mine will vibrate, so I'll know you're in trouble. It's synced to an app on my phone, so I can find you wherever you're at and come get you. If you're having a moment where you can't get to your meds, do the same thing, and I'll come to you and help."

My mouth sets in a firm line. I don't like this, but I can't say that. I know I cannot voice my frustration, because it's not technically with him. I am on edge about needing help from anybody. I can handle myself. I got this far without family and friends.

Then again, I lived with my full-time nurse before I moved back to Mayfield.

Rome seems to hear the current of disgruntlement that I will not voice. "Mine works the same way. If I am taken or if I need you, I do the same to mine, and yours will vibrate."

He rights the circle, so the hearts are together again, and sets it in my palm. Then he takes his own charm dangling from a white gold chain and twists it, setting off a noticeable vibration I can easily detect. Once he rights his, the vibration stops.

He closes my fingers around my charm, his chin lowered in submission because he knows this whole arrangement upsets me. "I need someone to have my back. I want you to know where I'm at in case one of the raids goes south, and I can't get out. How are you with a firearm?"

It takes me a second for his logic to sink in. This is for his protection also, not mine alone.

My lips part as I marvel up at him. He trusts me to get him out of tough situations. I'm his backup.

I swallow hard, this time enjoying the feel of his cool skin surrounding my fist while I hold onto the new piece of jewelry. "I'm the sheriff's daughter. I have four guns in various safes that I'll stash around the house once everything is settled."

"One in the salon?"

I scoff. "More than one."

"That's my girl." Rome pulls me into his arms, exhaling deeply when I allow my head to rest against his shoulder. His fingers feather through my brunette waves. "I'm going to sleep much better, now that I know you can watch out for me."

This flip of me looking out for him is not one that I expected. My chest puffs with pride that he trusts me with something as valuable as his safety.

My mind starts running down this new path, making plans along the way. "I need you to get me dried blood pellets. A few packs. I can't get them myself, but I should have them on hand in case I find you depleted."

I would just feed him my blood, but my blood is deadly to all vampires, so I wouldn't be much help to him in that situation.

Rome squeezes me tighter. "I'll arrange it." I can feel the protective angst in his embrace. "I hate that I can't offer you a safer life. I'm working on it. I'm doing all I can to clean up the West End. It's taking a lot longer than I anticipated. It's like every time we shut down a halluci-den, another pops up in its place." He kisses the top of my head. "I will make this city safe for you."

That's where my heart sinks. "See, that's the thing. My blood will always be this way. I won't ever be able to live without bulletproof glass and the looming threat of being abducted." I look up into his eyes, vulnerability shining through. "That's something you should know before this gets any more serious."

The corner of Rome's mouth lifts, fixing me with a wry half-smile that suggests I've said something amusing. "Do you think you can scare me away? I'm in this, Coletta."

The note of permanence shines in his beautiful blue eyes, reminding me that what we have cannot be easily blown away just because the world won't behave.

When his lips caress mine, all worry begins to leave my brain. His arm curls around my hips, coaxing my stomach to his. Oh, how I love the taste of Rome's cinnamon lips. His affection is silky and smooth, passionate and tender.

His hand sneaks down so he can trill his fingers up my thigh, stealing the moment for just the two of us while we have it. His touch climbs under my skirt while his tongue teases mine.

I love that I get this part of him to cherish and hold tightly in my heart.

And now I can protect the best parts of him, so he can come safely home to me.

2

THE FEAR OF THE VALENTINO MEN
ROME

Even a week after Colette was officially moved from her old home in the East End to her new place in Midtown, I am still looking over my shoulder for Fintan or her father to gun me down in broad daylight. But as that hasn't happened yet, I can only guess that Declan has done his part in keeping our relationship secret.

Declan's not half bad, actually. The medical profession gets zero training in treating vampires. While there are similarities, there are stark differences that could stand to be addressed. Whenever one of my men are badly injured, I either have Declan meet us in Midtown with his paramedic bag, so I can educate him on how to treat our kind, or I do a video chat with him, so he can learn remotely.

I've picked up a few things too, like how to get the stitching tighter when suturing a long tear from a knife fight. Orlando sits in on the calls, too. It's an alliance I did not expect, but I am no less grateful for it.

Nico is less than thrilled about the prospect of making nice with the enemy, as he calls them. My brother doesn't know of my infatuation with my sweet Coletta.

Orlando put his foot down that I must tell my baby brother tonight. I haven't stopped sweating all day.

I could tell him now, while Orlando drives us through West End with Nico in the backseat of my black sedan.

I could, but I'm not ready.

It's not going to go well, to say the least. Nico was enraged when I told him I was teaching Declan how to give medical attention to vampires. "They're not our kind, Rome. They're going to use that information against us. The humans are always looking for a way to get rid of vampires. You're playing into their hands!"

As much as I understand Nico's fears, which are not entirely unfounded, I trust my gut, which trusts Declan completely. I have known the guy since we were kids. He's not one to look for reasons to tear other people down.

Plus, Coletta adores him. I have to make nice with at least one member of her family. Declan is the easiest one to deal with.

Plus, it's no small boon to have a paramedic who is capable of treating us. We've never had proper medical care before. This could be the start of things actually changing for the better for my people. I know the world has a long way to go before vampires are considered more than a dangerous nuisance, but it's a start.

Declan seems to understand this, as well, so he's done his best to remain amiable, even though it is pretty clear I can't stop lusting after his kid sister.

That's another thing that is going to be a problem tonight when I tell Nico about my new girlfriend. Aside from us being different races, and her family spending years doing nothing to keep our territory safe when that was the sheriff's job, Coletta is Nico's age, which is a decade younger than me. She was just getting out of diapers when I hit my teen years.

I grimace at how cringeworthy that sounds, even in my own head. I will have to word it better than that.

"You're doing it again," Orlando scolds me. "Staring off into space, worrying without talking. What are we walking into that I don't know about?"

Oh, nothing more than Nico's flaring temper and smart mouth.

But I know that's not what Orlando is concerned about.

I tear my thoughts from the inevitable and refocus in on the matter at hand. "Martin's Dry Cleaning was only laundering the drug money on behalf of Frank's Grill. We need to figure out if the grill is where the sloppy drugs are originating from. If it's not Frank's Grill, then we need to dig beyond them."

The useful and often necessary drug called halluci-mend is what I cook up for my people, so we have some form of medicine that helps us. But that isn't the problem. Aside from cutting into our profit margins from creating and selling halluci-mend, the bastardized halluci-blend is far more addictive and can turn deadly if overused. Of course, the drug has been largely supplied in the West End, turning what could have been a thriving community into a depressing place to live.

If they cannot exterminate us, I guess their plan is to make us so miserable that we can't lift our heads to demand better from the world at large.

I have to figure out where the halluci-blend is coming from, so I can stop this drug from tearing down my people.

The stuff being sold in the East End isn't near as dangerous. Don't think that hasn't kept me up at night. It's a targeted aim at us.

"Awesome," Nico deadpans from the backseat. "Honestly, sometimes I'm on the sheriff's side. Might as well just let the idiots kill themselves. No one's forcing the B-level drugs on the populace. They're taking it of their own free will."

Nico only talks this disrespectfully to me when we're away from public view, as we are now while Orlando drives us through the West End.

I pause before I reach for the old response that I am sure my little brother has memorized by now. "Our halluci-mend is clean, but the halluci-blend is not. Our stuff is nothing like this garbage. Anything that makes a vampire's fangs fall out isn't something I want in my territory. Whoever is distributing this is playing on our misery, giving our people an escape that takes them further down the rabbit hole. There's no recovery for these people, Nico. They won't be able to kick their addiction; not that I've seen, at least."

Orlando's jaw tightens. "The West End can be better than this. I don't want vampires known for our unsafe streets and debilitating drug addictions. Do you?"

"No," Nico drones sulkily, sounding every bit like the child he is. "I'm just tired of this being *our* problem to handle. We're not the ones dealing this garbage."

"No arguments here," Orlando mumbles as he pulls into the parking lot of Frank's Grill. "Not too busy inside. Clear out the patrons before you get started, eh, Nico?"

My kid brother grunts, his fists moving in slow, clumsy swoops. "Caveman, smash! Nico no good for thinking jobs, only destroying things."

I roll my eyes at his sass. I wonder if I ever had the gall to talk back to Dad like that. "You want to do more of the talking and less of the smashing? Then go where I put you without a fuss. I had to do the same thing when Dad was grooming me. If you don't learn this skill, your first negotiation won't go anywhere, and you'll have to fight your way out anyway."

"Nico go where Rome says," my little brother replies,

still using the caveman cadence simply because he knows it annoys me.

"Take pride in your place in the family business, Nico. If you can't appreciate your role now, then you won't appreciate the people who you depend on when you're in charge someday."

Nico responds with an exasperated sigh. "Fine, fine. I'll be the most cheerful enforcer you've ever seen. Might even whistle a little tune while I demolish the valuables."

I am never more grateful for Orlando than when subjected to Nico's insufferable attitude. I swear, though Nico and Coletta are the same age, she is far more mature and capable than he is. She owns her own franchise, despite having dealt with a debilitating brain injury and a blood condition that puts a mark on her back. Nico wants everything handed to him, demanding the perks of our family name but not the grunt work it takes to maintain such a legacy.

He will learn.

But what a pain it is to teach him.

Orlando fists his door's handle. "I'll watch him, Rome."

That makes me feel a little better. The whole point of bringing along an enforcer is for me not to worry about anything except talking with the target.

3

FRANK'S BIG PROBLEM
ROME

I try to appear as if I am on top of my assets when I button my suit jacket and get out of the car. Orlando knows to walk ahead of me—the muscle making the first appearance to strike the appropriate amount of fear in my mark. Nico, however, makes to tag along at my side.

He has not earned it.

Orlando doesn't miss a beat, whistling like he's calling a dog. He motions to his side for Nico to quit being petulant already.

I mean, honestly.

Orlando and Nico enter ahead of me, each taking an exit to watch over like two gargoyles. The diners take notice, which is exactly what I want. People who have done nothing wrong can rest easy, knowing we are there to clean up any crime that has slipped under their noses. The others immediately begin to sweat because I am about to shut down the source of their halluci-blend.

I hope.

I don't enter because I don't need to. Orlando handles the work of getting the owner to come outside so we can speak without his patrons overhearing.

I lean against the red brick of the building, taking a cigar out of my pocket. I take my time lighting it because I am in no rush. He's the one with customers to get back to, not me. It's my job to make sure the vampires of my city don't succumb to a life in the gutter from which they can never escape.

I'm not even sure I like cigars, but it's part of the game. My father would start up a cigar when he began a shake-down, then put it out once the unpleasantries were over. My people know what to expect from my family, so I use my props as I understand them, even if I know I will have to rinse out my mouth before I will even attempt kissing my little cannoli.

I glance at the corner spot beside the sidewalk, my eyes catching on the bushes that are still perfectly manicured. Sure, I own this strip. I own most of the business property in the West End. That's the only reason our city has greenery that isn't overgrown or dead.

I probably fixate too much on the horticulture, but I can't help myself. I love it. Seeing pops of green sporadically throughout my end of the city gives me hope that one day, things might not be so grim. Each neatly trimmed bush and flower box is a promise I've made to myself that one day, the West End will be worthy of such beauty.

Frank comes out of his restaurant, harried and red-faced. His bald forehead is sweaty from working behind the grill all morning, coupled with the anxiety the guilty feel he no doubt is consumed with when my men walked into his establishment.

He mops his brow and dewy head with a stained rag. "To what do I owe the pleasure, Mister Valentino?"

It took a while after my father passed before my people stopped calling me by my first name, but they eventually fell in line.

"Seems we have a bit of a problem."

Frank gives an exasperated sigh. "Care to enlighten me? I've got a business to run."

Just for that insolence, I take two more puffs on my cigar before answering him.

I find a cigar helps keep my cool rhythm in an interrogation, rather than flying off the handle, as I am wont to do when people talk to me like I don't know up from down, or clean businesses from the dirty ones.

"Small world, the West End," I comment, letting the puffs of smoke fill the air between us. "So small that one might wonder just how orders are filled from business to business."

Frank is in his sixties. He spent decades answering to Dad, who answered to no one.

Not me. I answer to future generations of vampires who, I'm guessing, will want to walk down the streets safely someday.

Frank is silent now, no doubt sweating for a whole new reason.

"Funny thing about certain businesses around here. They seem to be ordering their staff lunches from you here at the Grill, but wouldn't you know, the employees bring their own lunches from home. Weird."

Frank ceases all movement. "I... which business is unsatisfied with their lunches?"

Nice dodge, but that's going to cost him.

I angle my head to peer into the front picture window of the restaurant and hold up one finger to Orlando.

We've been at this for so long; we don't need verbal requests.

I turn back around, my spine to the red brick. I puff on my cigar as shouts of fear erupt from the restaurant.

"How about this, Frank. Every time I ask you a question that you dodge, Orlando reminds you who owns this property you're lying to me on."

"What? I'm not lying. I don't know what you want me to say."

This time I don't bother putting my face in the window

to catch Orlando's eye. A simple thumb's up with my wrist visible to him is sufficient.

The sound of people screaming while Orlando goes to town on the tables and chairs isn't the best background noise while I smoke my cigar, but I'll take it.

Patrons race out of the restaurant, even though Orlando and Nico would never hurt them while teaching a miscreant a lesson. I take their flight as a compliment, dipping my head to a few of them as they run out into the autumn sunshine, screaming their alarm.

Ah, the fear of the Valentino family. Never gets old.

I don't have to look to know that no children are in attendance. That's the first move Orlando always makes before things get physical. He quietly asks all parents with young children to leave before things get rough. Doing this in the middle of the school day is just plain practical.

When Frank shouts his horror and tries to run into his business, Nico stops him at the entrance, as he should.

Good, Nico. You're learning.

Nico's hand on Frank's chest directs him back to the sidewalk. "Sorry, old man. This establishment is closed until you finish up your little chat."

Relaxation floods me, despite the chaos surrounding us. Nico might voice his disgruntlement with me behind closed doors, but when we're on the job, we present a united front.

I take another puff while Frank presses his nose to the

large front window, his hands splayed while he watches Orlando do what he does best.

"Make him stop!" Frank begs.

"I've already asked you my question, Frank. Orlando doesn't stop until I get my answer."

"What do you want to know? You want my list of businesses I deliver lunch to? Is that the big scandal that's worth all this?"

I despise being lied to, especially when the scene that's being painted to the patrons is that I am a shark coming to destroy local businesses. In reality, Frank is the one who is destroying our city. Frank is part of the reason their children can't play in the parks without fear of Halluci-junkies causing problems.

I will be damned if I let a broken city be our legacy.

I keep my cadence cool and unrushed. "I don't want a list of businesses you sell lunch to. I want the ones who give you money without getting food delivered. I'll bet it's a long list, Frank."

His eyes close, even as he is pressed up to the glass. "I don't know what you're talking about."

"Shame," I reply, and I truly mean it. "If hurting your business doesn't get the truth out of you, then we'll see how many of your fingers it'll take to get the real story on the table. You can work the grill one-handed, I'm sure." I wave my hand over my shoulder to his building. "Once you repair the damage, I mean."

Frank's rounded jaw ticks as sweat trickles down his temple. "What do you want me to say, Valentino? The product comes in and I'm supposed to get rid of it. The other business owners help me out because they know I'm stuck." He turns his face to me, looking stricken and scared of something other than the current trauma. "If I could wish my way out of this, I would, but I'm in too deep now."

Now we're getting somewhere. "In too deep with whom?"

Frank shakes his head. "If you think I'm not willing to lose my hand to a Valentino in order to keep my head from being taken off by..." He stops short before revealing the next level of the corrupt chain. "Do what you need to. I can't keep this up anymore. If I could get out of this nightmare, I would."

"Any reason you started up dealing halluci-blend in the first place?"

He flinches at the sound of his cash register cracking open.

This is when the real truth spills out. I can feel it. Though I don't understand his line of thought, he is too distressed by the sight of his business being demolished before his eyes to hold back.

"Talk," I demand, my cool demeanor falling to the wayside.

"Coming down on me, I guess I deserve it. But coming down on any of the other businesses I filter through is low. They've been by my side, trying to keep me from being killed. If I don't do what he says, I'll lose more than my business. More than my fingers. More than my life."

The lines under his eyes clue me in to something darker going on beneath the surface.

"Who's behind all this?" I lower my voice. "Frank, I can't help you if I don't know what I'm up against."

He scoffs, but the sound is more mournful than disrespectful. "You can't help me either way. And I don't know his name. No one does."

"What does he have on you?"

This time, his snort is in my direction. "You know so much about my business, but you know nothing about me."

I wait for more truth to come while a loud crash makes him shudder.

Frank's face pulls with true agony. "He has my son. If I don't do what he says and push the product, my son dies."

My stomach hollows in time with my chest tightening. "How long has your son been missing? Why didn't I hear about this?"

Frank's scowl tightens. "What could you have done? What could anyone have done? I have no name to search for, no lead on where he might be. The news doesn't care about missing vampire children. No one cares."

If I wasn't a vampire, I would suggest the police, but

because Frank and I are considered sub-citizens, I know there are precious few options.

I turn to peer into the picture window, signaling for Orlando to stop.

Frank closes his eyes. "No. Tear it apart. If he's watching, he can't know I told you about him. If he thinks I went to you, my son and I are as good as dead."

"Is he monitoring your phone calls?"

"Yes."

"How long has this been going on?"

Frank meets my eyes with gravity I cannot begin to understand. "How long do you think?"

My jaw firms. "Since the peace treaty went into effect?"

Frank closes his eyes and presses his forehead to the glass. "They'll keep us down one way or another."

His words are telling. "The man who stole your son—it's a human? It's not a vampire?"

"From what I can gather, yes. I can't be sure, though."

I glance around surreptitiously. "Okay, you're right. We shouldn't be seen getting along. But I'll leave money to pay for the damages in your bathroom. You tell all your connections I shook you down real hard and you didn't crack. I know nothing about your son or that you're a fence. You were late on your rent, and that's why I stopped by."

Frank turns his head back to stare at me, his mouth open in wonder. "Are you going to help me?"

I fight the urge to hug this poor man. "I'll do some digging far away from you, so this doesn't blow back on your son. But I'll need more information. Where can we meet?"

I am used to men crying. They usually do before they take a fatal bullet. But when Frank's eyes well up, it does something to my heart.

My father would walk away right about now. He wouldn't promise to help a hopeless situation. When Nico was taken by a few dealers who were discontent with their cut, Dad was angry they'd disrespected him. He didn't shed a single tear.

I could never be a father. I would be paralyzed with worry. I couldn't bring myself to be as cold and calculating as my own father, but I know that if I cared as much as Frank, I would be one of those hovering parents who never lets their kid go anywhere without a bodyguard.

Orlando. I could trust Orlando with my child. No one else.

I shake my head at myself. It's a moot point. I will never reproduce. I would be a terrible father. Plus, I would need to pair up with a vampire woman to make that possible, and I have eyes for no one but my sweet Coletta.

Damn it. I don't want to care what happens to this boy, but now I have to get to the bottom of this, so Frank can have his son back.

Frank is a caring father—so much that he is willing to throw away the entire city to get him back.

My father never did that for me.

Frank and I work out a time and place where we can talk in private. Then I go inside and set a fair amount of cash on the sink of the bathroom.

Orlando and Nico exit the building and move to the parking lot, but I meet Frank's eyes once more. "I will help you, Frank."

His lower lip quivers, which is a sight I know I won't be able to shake anytime soon.

Orlando and Nico ask me if I got any information when I slide into the car with them.

"Nothing interesting," I lie. Though, I catch Orlando's eye, letting him know I am in way over my head.

4

THE DANCE WE DO

COLETTE

There are few things more satisfying than working a full day at a business I own, making sure all my stylists earn well above what they need to meet their basic bills. We all go home with exhausted smiles, smelling like sweat and shampoo.

The new house on Cherry Cove doesn't feel entirely mine yet, but I've only been living here two weeks. Much of that time has been spent unpacking and setting up rooms for optimum efficiency. I'm not sure I've learned how to rest in my home just yet.

Fortunately, this is a lesson I am determined tonight to learn.

My shower is longer than it needs to be, but I take my time indulging in the hot water. Working in high heels when you're on your feet all day is a poor choice, but my pride needs the vote of confidence. I would rather be in pain, my legs bragging because they have sensation and are mobile than admit to the world (and myself) that there are days when my body betrays me.

Today was not that day. Today I sashayed around the salon, sweeping, cutting, curling and whistling because I am the luckiest girl in the world.

My doctor said I would never be able to live on my own, yet here I am.

My doctor said I wouldn't be able to get around without a walker for several years, if ever.

I dance now.

Not well, of course, but I dance well enough not to be kicked out of my own salon. And after the phone call I received today, I wouldn't put it past my good luck if I actually did possess fantastical mythological powers (other than the one that kills vampires).

I dry off, still with plenty of time before Rome is supposed to come by for dinner. Though it's nearly seven o'clock, neither of us eat dinner without the other anymore. Our schedules are so cattywampus that if we don't force time to stand still, it never does.

Having dinner with Rome every night is a big step up from only having one day a week that I can see him.

I throw on a pale pink and white sun dress. Even though it's crisp outside, I am not ready to put away my summer clothes.

Being stubborn against even the sun isn't my wisest

move, but a chill is worth the price of spaghetti straps holding up a breezy midthigh-length dress. I love the blush lace that lines the hem. The thing is utterly feminine, which is another piece of independence I have clung to. Being the only female in a house with two Alpha males and Declan meant that every scrap of pink that made it in past the front door was a victory.

The casserole I threw into the oven before I hopped in the shower has two minutes left on the timer. I wind my damp shoulder-length brown waves up atop my head in a bun and set the table. Even though Rome would be more than happy to eat at the counter on the tall stools, a little civility is the bare minimum of what our time together deserves.

I go one further and pull out my mother's wedding China. It makes me sad to see such pretty plates tucked away in a dark box somewhere no one can appreciate them. I use a stool to take down the box of delicate dishes, admiring each piece as I pull it out and set it at the table.

So pretty. It's not my taste, but that hardly matters. With my mother's China on my table, I can pretend she is with me. I never met her, since she died in childbirth, but there are enough news clippings of her life for me to assemble a reasonable conjuring of the wonderful woman she must have been.

I wonder if she would approve of Rome. I wonder if she and I would have been close enough to where her approval would actually hold weight, or if she would be just another family member from whom I would hide my relationship.

Melancholy hits me at just the wrong moment as I turn down the illumination overhead and light two tall white taper candles in the center of the table. I hear the garage opening, so I roll my shoulders back, pretending I have never experienced anything shy of sheer fabulousness. I'm not sure if I am pretending for Rome or for myself.

Even though I still feel new to my own house, I love that Rome is at home wherever he exists, including here. He comes in through the side door off the kitchen that attaches to the garage, already taking off his suit jacket.

His shoulders lower as he exhales. Whatever stress he held onto before entering my home, I can tell he has left it outside our haven for the evening.

"It smells amazing in here. Tré-sur, what have you been up to? I thought you were working all day. When did you have time to cook?"

I set down a saucer and clear the gap between us to indulge in a small slip of a kiss. "I threw it together this morning before work and put it in the oven when I got home."

He tastes like cigars, which isn't a normal occurrence.

"Angel," he breathes, stroking the apple of my cheek. Our kiss takes a pause so we can admire each other up close.

There's something sad behind his wistful expression

tonight. He always regards me as if I am something precious and breakable, but tonight, he looks positively wary of harming me. Like he's afraid to touch my skin harder than a whisper.

"Rome, are you alright?"

He hesitates before responding, drinking in my features as if he hasn't seen me in months. The strain makes him look like he is in pain, though his voice is low and steady. "I'm fine, Coletta. Just missed your face, is all."

Alarms go off in my mind. "Are you bleeding? What happened? You never say 'I'm fine' unless something horrible has happened. Let me call Declan. He can give you a look."

Rome staves off my fretting by pressing his lips to mine. Before my lashes sweep shut, I catch sight of the pained look in his squinched eyes. It's as if he has been starving for days, and our kiss is the only thing keeping him upright and fed.

So I indulge him (and myself) for the moment, leaning into the kiss. My hands roam his body slowly, caressing as they are wont to do whenever he is near. Only this time, they aren't touching his musculature strictly for pleasure.

I need to make sure he is okay.

My palms stroke down his sides, measuring his tightness of breath when I touch down on his right hip.

Bruise.

When our kiss comes to a crest, we slow in pitters and

patters of affection, tasting and appreciating what we can only enjoy in private.

"Did you miss me?" he asks in a low voice as he starts up a slow dance.

"I just cried the day away missing your face, useless for all other things."

Rome chuckles. "I'll bet."

He takes his time twirling me out and then winding my body back to his.

It's romantic, sure, but it's a test. Just as I patted him down to check for minor and major assaults, our little slow dance is his way of testing my movements to see how stiff my body has become. He wants to make sure I am taking my daily meds, but asking me outright isn't the way to go.

Flickers from the tall tapers at the table light his beautiful olive skin, making him appear otherworldly, and like a prince this universe doesn't deserve.

We are the same animal, too prideful to admit our weaknesses. Yet he lets me pat him down, and I allow him him twirl me, so I know we both want our underbellies exposed only to each other. Admitting those horrors to ourselves—that vulnerability might not be such a bad thing in the right hands—isn't something either of us are willing to do just yet.

So we kiss and dance until the day comes that we can check on each other without it being an affront to our precious pride.

Hopefully we'll still kiss and dance when the need to salvage our pride is not an issue anymore.

Rome must have noticed my wrist and forearm being uncooperative, because he massages it as we trade tiny kisses while we dance. I'm not tremoring, but my limbs are stiffer than I would like.

I love that he takes good care of me.

I loathe that I need the help.

Rome keeps his eyes on my wrist. "Can I request no work talk tonight? I had a lousy day, and I could use a break from it all."

I brush my nose across his. "What a coincidence. I was just going to ask you if you could read to me tonight. I love it over the phone, but I have it on good authority that you're even more irresistible when you read to me in person."

Rome looks so relieved that my heart aches to ask him what went wrong with work, and how can I fix it. "Thank you, tré-sur. What did you cook for us?"

I wonder when the last time was that he ate a proper meal. "A casserole and a salad."

He peers over my shoulder. "You lit candles."

"I did."

His kiss takes a darker turn, his tongue sweeping across mine as his arms tighten around me.

I love this. I love everything about his body warming mine. Though my movements are generally stiffer at the end of a workday, in his arms, I feel like a ballerina fresh off a pirouette.

How I lived for so long without this is a wonder I still can't wrap my mind around. He holds me like I matter, his kiss delving into the deeper parts of me that I usually keep locked behind closed doors.

But I open myself up for him, welcoming the pillaging because surrender sounds like the sweetest promise.

When the kiss comes to a crest, his hand drifts to my collarbone. He's been doing this more often, his fingers fondling the necklace he gave me. It's his reminder that I am safe—a vow that I will not vanish from his life.

I see a flash of worry flicker in his eyes, stealing his certainty with a breath of fear. I don't want to instill more unrest in him. I want our relationship to be a relief, not a stressor.

"I'm okay," I assure him between light pecks and nose nuzzles.

He leans his forehead to mine, his cigar-tainted breath bathing my nose. "For the record, this is why I didn't date. It's like a heart attack waiting to happen. I think too much about everything that could go wrong."

I kiss his lips once more and then sit him down at the table. Instead of taking my seat across from him, I stand behind his chair so I can run my fingers through his hair.

There are a few things all hairstylists are masters at, one of which being scalp massages.

I can reassure Rome all night long, but nothing is going to leech the poison of stress from him like me manually massaging it from his head. He has thick, obsidian hair that begs me to feather my fingers through it.

A guttural groan escapes him as his shoulders slump. I allow myself a self-satisfied smirk. I love that I can help him unwind.

I keep the massage going for a few minutes until the smell of tomato, cheese and oregano with noodles is too enticing to ignore. Then I move to the freezer and grab out one of my many ice packs. I don't want to embarrass Rome, but he needs to baby his bruising a bit if he wants to be fully functional in the morning. I kiss his cheek as I press the ice pack to his hip.

He hisses and bites on his lower lip. "It's fine, Coletta. I heal faster than a human."

"I'm counting on it. That's why I'm only insisting on an ice pack, rather than you lying down or me calling Declan to come give you a look."

I know it's a struggle, but Rome allows me to look after him. It's the only way this will work. We must have equal displays of vulnerability and trust. I don't want Rome: The Bull Who is Always in Charge. I want a partner.

The more he shows me his underbelly, the more I might someday stop cringing when my own weaknesses come to light in his presence.

Before I find my seat, Rome brings my palm to his lips,

placing a kiss there for me to hold onto. It's a small moment, but it's ours. I hold his appreciation for us in my hand and promise silently that I will be careful with us.

I open my mouth to ask him about his day, but the sound of the doorbell stiffens my spine.

Rome stands. "Were you expecting a delivery?" His hand is on the hilt of his gun.

Whatever relaxation my scalp massage granted him is gone now.

"No. I'll go see who it is." Mine is the only house on the dead-end street. No one stops by unannounced or uninvited.

Rome is out of his seat and moving toward the door. He peers though the peephole and turns to me with pure horror on his face. "Did you invite your father over?"

His whisper takes a second to register in my mind. My eyes widen with panic. "What? No!" I wave Rome out of the way. "You have to hide."

Hurt flickers across his features. "He should know about us."

I blanch. "That is your worst idea yet." I'm glad Rome parked in my garage.

Rome kisses my cheek and then flits soundlessly to the end of the hall, shutting himself in one of the rooms. I give him a good ten seconds to find a hiding place before I open the front door.

This is going to be a disaster.

5

MY FATHER IN MY HOUSE
COLETTE

When the front door swings open, I try not to look as if I am hiding a vampire in my home. "Sheriff? What a surprise to see you here. Did you need something?"

My father looks just as flustered as I feel. "Does a father need a reason to visit his daughter? Seems if I waited around for an invitation, I might be waiting forever."

I grimace at the not-so-subtle guilt trip. Was I supposed to invite him over? He never showed an interest in wanting to be in my space before.

"Um, come on in, I guess." The second he steps inside, my teenaged worries start to take over. Did I leave dirty laundry out? Is there dust on the mantle? Are there dishes in the sink? These are things my father notices. He ran a tight ship growing up, which translated into all three of us kids needing to have immaculately clean homes.

When he takes his shoes off and steps further in, dread courses through my veins.

It's not the threat of the mess I should be worried about; it's the nicely laden dinner table, complete with lit candles. All that's missing are scattered rose petals to christen it as a perfectly set romantic evening.

My father winces, chagrinned at the sight. "Oh! Were you expecting someone? Am I interrupting something?"

The hopeful note in his voice makes me cringe. He doesn't want me to find happiness or a partner. He wants me to get knocked up so the Deadblood legacy can continue. In which case, the candles wouldn't be romantic, but more of a fertility ritual.

Gross.

I pull a fresh lie out of my hat. "No, nothing like that. Rachel is coming over later. One of my stylists. I just set the table nice because we've been working hard this week and could use a little elegance."

I'm not sure if the sheriff buys my lie, but at least he doesn't press further.

Very unlike him, actually.

He lifts the corner of one of the plates, examining the design of green ivy surrounding gold swirls on the rim. "I forgot you took these. Haven't seen them in ages."

There's a tenderness to my father as he touches the

dish that never saw the outside of the cupboard when they were in my childhood home. We don't talk about my mother. Not like I would have much to add. I have zero memories of the woman.

Every woman with the Deadblood gene doesn't have a typical lifespan. Mom made it to thirty before her muscles began to atrophy.

She made it through her last pregnancy, but didn't live to see her legacy continued.

Don't think that doesn't haunt me.

I bury that condemnation as quickly as it comes, refusing to claim the expected shortening of her life as my own.

"Rachel's running late, actually," I offer. "She should be here soon."

My father shakes his head and sets down the plate. "You and Rachel do this often?"

I clear my throat. "Not often enough."

He speaks slowly, as if he is uncertain what should be said. "Should I… meet her?"

I'm not sure where he's going with this. "You have met her. She works in the salon. She's the branch manager, actually. I'll introduce you the next time you come in."

"I'd like that." He motions around the house, feigning ease. "So, show me around. It looks nice in here. I can't believe how moved in you are already. I expected to show up and help you unpack a few boxes."

My father was going to help me? That's a first.

I debate pointing that out but figure it's best to keep my mouth shut if I want him to leave sooner rather than later.

"Oh, Declan and the movers helped with that." It's partially true. Rome, Declan and Orlando were my movers, and they were plenty helpful.

My father turns to me with sadness painting his features. I don't understand it. I don't understand any of this. Why he's even here is a mystery. "I guess you don't need my help anymore," he rasps.

His hair is thinning, showcasing more than one bald spot where there used to be light brown curls. His thick neck has sagging skin that makes him look older than his sixty years.

Melancholy strikes my heart. My father's help usually involves hiding me away while he does the grownup work in the city without me.

I should tell him to leave. I am certain Rome does not appreciate having to disappear for this long.

"You okay, Sheriff?" I ask in a quiet voice. I know the answer before it comes. I'm not sure why I even asked in the first place.

"Of course. I'm always fine." My father slaps his hands together. "I breezed through the living room. Show me around? Make me feel like I know my daughter."

His phrase is strange and oddly sweet, which is how I know I must have misheard him. I do as he asks, though, showing off the décor around the fireplace, the throw pillows that match the light blue walls perfectly, and the coffee table Declan bought me as a housewarming gift.

"Declan's been here?" the sheriff asks, sounding hurt.

"Of course. He helped me unpack." *I just told you as much.*

"I'm glad you two have each other. You always were good at looking out for each other."

"Sure. You have Fintan. I have Declan. We've got our zones."

My father frowns. "I guess that's true. I know Fintan wishes he were closer with you."

Well, that's an obvious lie. Fintan doesn't care about anything other than himself, money and pleasing dear old Dad.

And controlling me.

My brows push together. "Why are we talking about this? You never cared how we all got along. Fintan and I are fine. I respect him as much as any man who tries to control a woman's uterus against her wishes."

Maybe that was a little too direct. But in my defense, I found out a few weeks ago that my eldest brother was setting me up on blind dates and charging the men who wanted to take me out twenty thousand dollars for the opportunity.

Fintan still doesn't know that I am aware of his side

hustle, but as far as phantom familial affections are concerned, I am done with him.

My father's mouth firms. "Fintan's got opinions, that's for sure."

It's the most I've ever heard the sheriff express anything close to displeasure regarding the golden child of the family.

I stand in front of the cream-colored leather couch, my hand on my hip. "And you don't share Fintan's opinions? You don't think I should continue the bloodline as soon as possible?"

My father runs his hand over his face, looking ancient and tired from too much life and not enough living. "I don't know what I think anymore. Is it too strange to just want you to be happy?"

My fight face comes out as I brace myself for a verbal brawl. "You've never given a crap about my happiness. What is this? What are you really doing here? If you're trying to inspect my home to make sure the locks are secure, Declan already did that."

My father's expression firms with displeasure. "Fine. Glad to hear it." Instead of going to the exit, he turns down the hall. "Do you need help setting up in the rooms back here?"

Panic rises in my throat, since I'm pretty sure that is the direction Rome headed to hide out. "I told you; Declan already helped with that."

"Well, since I'm not going to be invited over, this might be the only time I get to see my daughter's home."

He opens the door to my office, which has a sleeper sofa up against the far wall. I got that for the nights Declan stays over. The sheriff grunts at the spare room, no doubt finding nothing negative on which he can comment.

My frustration begins to bubble over. "If you wanted a different relationship, you should have done things differently. You can't stomp around all mopey because things turned out exactly how you orchestrated them."

The sheriff's head swings in my direction, his overgrown brows pushed together. "And how is that?"

"Are you serious?" I talk with my hands when I am frustrated, so my arms are in full swing, even though my wrists are stiff. "You put an ocean between us when I was sick. Most parents might cling tighter when their daughter is kidnapped, but you sent me completely out of your sight. Now you want an invitation into my home? For what? You never wanted to be in my life before. Why do you care now?" I cross my arms. "You're working an angle. I want to know what it is before I find my things packed up and my address suddenly changed without my consent." A second wave of rage flares. "Which, incidentally, you can't do anymore. You don't have power of attorney now, and I'm over eighteen. So however you're thinking of getting me out of your sight this time, it had better involve a body bag, because I am not moving from Mayfield."

6

FAMILY FEUD

COLETTE

My father regards me as if I am being a petulant teenager, throwing a fit over the length of my miniskirt. "We're doing this now? Having it out over an issue that died years ago?"

My mouth falls open, making it clear that this was the wrong thing to say. Perhaps it was a decade ago that he sent me away, but every day, it stung afresh. Declan and I were inseparable, even with an ocean between us. We talked every day while I was overseas. Other than his phone calls, I had no one but my nurse for a long time. "You hardly ever called, and when you did, you only spoke to my nurse. You didn't visit me. You sent me away and wanted nothing to do with me. Now you want to come into my home?"

My father's jaw tightens. "I suppose I deserve that."

"You deserve worse than that and more than the

lecture I am giving you. You don't deserve to be let in the front door. Fortunately, I turned out nothing like you."

It's mean, sure. It's a low blow that I don't want to regret, but the second my words hit the air, I do.

Then again, maybe I am more like him than I realized. I hurt him without thinking of his heart, of how my words would cut the tender flesh that used to be stone.

He let down his armor for me, and I ran him through because I could.

My father's hands slide into his pockets, taking a submissive demeanor that looks entirely foreign on him. Where was this man growing up? "What should I have done, Coco?"

Heat flares in my cheeks as fury raises my volume. "You shouldn't have sent me away from my family!"

I expect an argument, because that's been his personality my whole life. Instead, he humbles himself for reasons I cannot begin to fathom. He keeps his chin lowered. "You're right. I should have gone with you. Maybe I should have moved our whole family."

I go silent, taking a step back. I don't know what's gotten into my father. I am never right in his eyes. I never have a valid point.

When it's clear I won't fill in the gaps of the conversation, my father stands in the middle of my office with a look so forlorn, I instantly want to take back any of my words that have hurt him.

"I should have left Mayfield and taken the boys overseas with you. I wasn't thinking straight. I was scared, Coco." He pauses, and for a glimmer of a second, he lets me see the true fear that haunts him still. "All I could focus on was getting you out of the city. Three abductions. *Three.* If we're counting up the ways I've failed you, not getting out of Mayfield after your first kidnapping is the one I kick myself over the most. Second is not tracking down the doctor who worked miracles on you sooner. Maybe your mother would still be alive if I had. She was in agony every night when she was your age, but you are still filled with life and grace."

Beneath the shock, I begin to wonder if there has been a neurological event inside my father's brain. "Are you having a stroke or something? Why are you being nice?"

The sheriff hangs his head, but instead of answering me, he keeps going. "I thought my job was to clean up Mayfield so it would be safe for you one day. Then I got carried away with that and arrested a disproportionate amount of vampires, creating a whole new problem." He purses his lips as if praying for the right words. "I was your sheriff instead of your father. I made the wrong call. Now I see you out there opening another branch of your business, creating your shampoos and whatnot, and not needing me for a single thing." He lets out a joyless laugh. "And I orchestrated it to turn out like this. I just didn't realize what I was doing until it was too late." He motions to my guarded expression. "Until you started looking at me like that."

I don't understand. Or maybe the part of me that's been secretly wishing for a father who wanted a relationship with me understands his words, but the realist who corrupts my heart tells me it could all be a trap.

My body doesn't move an inch, as if I am facing a predator who might strike the moment my guard is down. "You're not here to try to force me out of Mayfield?"

My father shakes his head. "No, Coco. I'm here to try and force my way into your life, apparently. Though I have no right to ask for such a thing." He motions around my office and toward the hallway. "It's clear you don't need me. Maybe that's good. Sometimes my help isn't all that helpful. That's the wisdom of old age, I guess."

At this, I finally find my voice, tremulous though it may be. "Of course I need you. I've needed you for years. But you weren't there, so I learned to get by without having all that I needed."

My father's chin lifts. He sits down in my chair at my desk, his hands folding over his slightly pooched belly. "What is it you need? Maybe I can get better at helping if you can take a chance and tell me *how* I should help you." He motions between the two of us. "We both budge a little. I wait for you to tell me what you need, instead of taking over, and you gather up the courage to tell me and trust that I'll try to be there for you without ruining your life."

Moisture wells in my eyes. My throat suddenly hurts, raw with unspoken emotion. I don't trust him; I have no reason to. However, I don't want to kick him out the way he abandoned me. I don't want to hate myself the same way I loathed him for so many years.

I don't know if I believe he can or will actually listen, but I know that if I don't take this chance, someday I might regret it.

"I don't want help," I admit. "My pride runs just as deep as yours."

My father snorts but doesn't take offense.

My voice is quiet, afraid of cracking the offer of peace if I put any pressure on it to test its veracity. "What I want, you might not be able to give me."

"Try me. Please, Coco. You're right; I might be terrible at being your father, but I'd like to try. Even if it's too late, I want to try."

It's way too late, and he won't be able to do what I need.

But if I could take a chance and ask one thing of the man who tried to raise me and failed, it would be this.

"I want you to listen without fixing. I don't think you know how to do that."

My father's bulbous nose scrunches as if he has come across a foul smell. His mouth pulls like he's eaten something sour, and for a second, I think he is going to get up and leave.

Instead, he leans back in his seat, running his hand

over his face. "You're right. I don't know how to do that. But I can try."

It's a strange dance we do, sizing each other up in the midst of a double whammy of sheer vulnerability (which neither of us are skilled at).

I swallow hard, knowing it's now or never. My confession comes out in a choked whisper. "I'm seeing someone. I'm not ready to tell you who just yet, but I'm happy with this person."

To his credit, the sheriff purses his lips instead of taking over. I can tell his next words are a struggle. "Good for you, Coco. That's real good." He clears his throat, wiping his palms on his thighs. "I suppose asking if I can meet your special person would be overstepping."

"For now, I think it's best my private life stays private. You wouldn't approve."

Defiance much like my own blazes in my father's eyes. "How do you know that?"

My hand begins to tremble. My nerves are running too high to last much longer in this conversation without taking another pill. My meds last me well enough through a normal day, but my father is acting anything but normal tonight.

"I know you won't like me seeing this person for a number of reasons. One of those reasons is that I can't have children with them." I close my eyes, wishing I didn't have to have this conversation with myself, much less aloud with my father. However, the moment the words hit the air, I realize how devastating they are. Being with Rome means never having children of my own. Though there are obvious reasons why I should never procreate, being that my deadly blood would be passed down if I have a girl, every now and then when I am honest with myself, I wish silently that I could have children.

But that is a danger to the world I would never risk.

My father must sense the heartbreak and stunned uncertainty on my face, because he handles my raw emotions with care instead of an iron fist with all the answers.

"Is this person good to you?" he finally asks.

Tears well in my eyes and cascade down my cheeks with a blink. My voice is barely audible. "So good, I can barely believe it's real."

Silence spreads out between us, which is the best sound I could hope for. The sheriff isn't rushing in to control the situation. He isn't offering advice or telling me what to do with my body.

I have never known this side of him before, but I like it.

He leans forward, his elbows on his thighs. "It was like that for me when I met your mother."

I go completely still. We never talk about her.

"I knew that having children with her would be a risk. A statement. I knew that her own mother didn't live beyond thirty." He shakes his head, his eyes far away as if seeing the lovely visage of my mother all over again. "But I couldn't help myself. I was a fool for her, and happy for the privilege. Those other complications didn't seem all that important, to be honest. We had you three because we wanted three kids, not for any sort of genocidal reason." He takes his time breathing in deep and then exhales as if he has carried more than his share of grief for an unending number of years. "If this is the person you love, then I am happy for you. Kids or not. Whether you'll let me meet your special person or not."

I have no idea what to say to that, so my tears do most of the talking. "You won't like my special person," I admit through my sniffles.

The sheriff chuckles. "I think that comes standard, no matter who you choose. I'm the father. I'm supposed to think no one is good enough for my little girl." He holds up his hands. "But I'll try to be good if you ever do bring your person by." He holds my watery gaze. "Truly, Coco. I can get better at being your father. Look at me, not jumping in and demanding all the answers. You held up your end by trying to trust me, and I'm holding up my end by not controlling you. We can do this."

I snicker as I swipe at my eyes. "I hardly recognize you." I sniffle as more tears come. I didn't realize how badly I've been wanting a parent who can just know me without controlling me. "Thank you. Truly."

My father stands, glancing around my office. "Is it

controlling or overstepping for me to tell Fintan not to make you go on those blind dates anymore?"

I smile up at him, surprised my mouth knows how to do that in his towering presence. "I wouldn't mind that, actually. I really hate them."

"I can imagine." His expression sobers. "You pretend a lot for us, don't you. Pretend to be happy. Pretend to give these dates a chance just to pacify us." When I don't answer—I mean, I'm not sure what he's expecting me to say—he rubs his chin. "Well, no more. Fintan and I will stay out of your personal life until you tell us we're allowed in. And for the record, I do want to meet your special friend. I won't even try to intimidate them. I'll be good. My gun will stay in its holster." He holds up his hands when I start to tell him I'm not ready for them to meet yet (or ever). "I'll also be patient. No rush. I trust you."

I balk at him, unsure if he's ever said that before to anyone, much less me. "What did you just say?"

His bushy brows bunch together, as if he can't remember which part of his piece hit me hardest. "That I trust you?"

I nod, locking the sound of those words in my memory in case I can't believe they happened in the morning.

Trust isn't a thing in our family, except for between Declan and me. And even that comes tentatively. I didn't tell Declan about Rome; he found out. Declan didn't tell me he was gay; I guessed, and he confirmed, back when he was a teenager, and life started to paint a clearer picture of my brother to me.

The sheriff still doesn't know his own son is gay. Trust isn't a credo our family has ever lived by.

My father trusts me.

And I am in love with a vampire.

The sheriff doesn't do more than glance inside my bedroom, which is a relief. Rome is most likely in the closet, holding his breath and trying to think invisible thoughts.

I follow my father to the front door, my hands shaking more than usual. I shove them behind my back, as if they are covered in mud from playing outside with Nino-bear when I wasn't supposed to get dirty.

"Thanks for stopping by," I offer as my father fists the handle.

"Thanks for letting me in the front door. I'll call first next time."

I gnaw on my lower lip, deciding on a whim to take a chance, even if it makes no sense to try. "Maybe I'll invite you over instead. The fifteenth? I'll show you the backyard. It's real nice. Maybe you can help me plant some bushes before the ground frosts over."

My father's shoulders sag, as if that's the one thing he has wanted to hear. "You want me in your space?"

"I don't know," I admit. "But if you show up like this, I don't think I'd mind it."

We aren't the touchy-feely type of family, so there aren't hugs on his way out.

The second my father exits, I close the door and slide to the floor, catching my sobs in my hand.

I don't know how or why that just happened, but I think I finally got a glimpse of the father I always wanted.

7

PUSHING MY BUSINESS
COLETTE

Rome has been careful with me more than usual since he was privy to an alien taking over my father and granting him a whole new personality. Last night after he came out of the closet once the coast was clear, Rome ran a hot bath for me and fixed me a plate of food. He found my medication to stop my hands from trembling. He didn't lecture me about missing out on the perfect opportunity to tell my father about us. He simply stayed with me while my world shifted and became strange. Even now as I bottle the shampoo I made this morning, I am grateful for Rome, and even my father.

It's silly to be nervous about a phone call, but this is one I've been putting off for quite some time. The salon is bustling outside my office, but I am tethered behind my desk, staring at my phone and playing a childish game of chicken.

I can do this.

If I am going to go all in on chasing my career dreams to the fullest, I might as well stop selling myself short.

The first business on my list isn't willing to take a meeting, and neither are the next eight. I don't use my real name, nor have I told Rome about my ambition to sell my patented line of haircare products in retail stores. In fact, in my office making these phone calls is the first time I say aloud what I truly want out of life.

I start with local businesses, grateful when the tenth store in Mayfield that sells high end products takes my phone call and entertains the notion of me sending them samples.

I don't want a simple contract. Anyone can get that if they make enough phone calls. I want the people selling them to love them so much that they can't stop recommending them to their patrons. I want true brand loyalty that has nothing to do with the racism my name tends to drum up.

Opening a salon in Midtown was a statement, a line in the sand that we will not be at war with the vampires of the world.

But launching my own brand of shampoos and conditioners? That's got nothing to do with politics; that's all me.

Just me.

If it fails, I will experience it all as a normal woman might, with no safety net and no giant statement to go with the product, other than "Hey, this will make your hair routine less of a pain."

It takes forty-three phone calls, but I finally make progress.

By the time my first haircut and style of the day arrives, fourteen store managers in and around Mayfield have agreed to take my samples and personally use them for a week. If they like them, then we can talk doing business together.

It's a rush of adrenaline, cold calling and doing the grunt work of pursuing my dream, but when it is over, my smile cannot be helped.

I did it. I bet on myself with no backup. I didn't use my celebrity that might open doors which should remain closed. No one who does business with me will sell my products in my store because of who I am; they will either love the product and push it, or they won't. It will be a genuine success or a true failure.

The salon takes hardly any time at all to fill itself with the usual hum of gossip and laughter. Victor's shaves are booked through the day, and Rachel's miraculous coloring abilities are in high demand. In fact, she is so talented that people who came in for a wash and cut end up requesting to add highlights or a whole new color to their appointment when they see the wonders she works on the client in her chair.

Assisting Rachel is no big deal, but she acts like I've

saved her firstborn from drowning when I mix colors for her so she can tend to her client with two hands and undivided focus.

I don't exactly have a ton of time to greet my father when he drops in unannounced, but I make the effort all the same. "Hello, Sheriff. Did I forget something? Is it your day to meet with the Valentinos?"

I worry that if I say Rome's name aloud in the presence of my father, he will know for certain that I let his former nemesis unbutton my blouse last night.

He will know that Rome's capable hands slid over every inch of my body, and I was begging for more.

My cheeks flame when I recall the hunger in Rome's eyes the moment he took in my lacey lavender bra.

My father motions to Victor. "I made an appointment for a shave." He dips his chin toward me. "Is that okay? I promise not to hover."

The corner of my mouth crooks at the cuteness. This dance we are doing is difficult and filled with rules neither of us are certain of, but we are trying anyway, even if we get it wrong.

"That's more than fine. You're in for a real treat. Victor is the best at what he does."

Victor blows me a kiss and escorts my father to his chair. "She's not wrong. How's your morning been so far, Sheriff?"

"Oh, nothing too crazy. Defused a few bombs, directed

the SWAT team, convinced a jumper there was still meaning in life, rescued a kid from a well. The usual."

Victor chuckles, the brunette bun atop his head motionless even though he is full of constant movement.

It's strange to have no animosity while in such close proximity with my father. Usually, I am boiling with unspoken resentment. I'm sure some of that is still lurking, but I am on such a high from my victory this morning, and our breakthrough last night, that his presence doesn't bother me at all. In fact, I kind of like that he's here.

He makes friendly chatter with Rachel and Victor while I take my next client, making sure to finish her up before I need to run my errands.

It shouldn't be a secret, really. It's not like I am doing anything earthshattering. But expanding my business like this is important to me. I could open another branch, once I break in Rachel so she can fully take over as manager, but I want to do something different. I don't want to put all my eggs in one basket with the Kennedy Salon franchise.

Once I am caught up on the people who need styling, I spend far too much time on the lilac-hued boxes. I make sure the wrapping is high end and tells a story of sophistication without pretention. The people of Mayfield should have nice things that they see first before the rest of the world gets a crack at it.

When I load my deliveries into my trunk on my lunch break, I feel ready for this new adventure.

It's when I go to sit down in the driver's seat that my blood runs cold.

Locked. My car was locked with the alarm set. Only Declan has the spare set of keys, in case I lose mine or can't manage the dexterity to get myself home.

So then how is there a note, written in the same typed script as the other that Fintan shoved in my face at the last family dinner, resting on my seat?

My mouth is dry as I pick up the letter with my name on it. Sweat stings my upper lip as I take in the words of a mind gone clearly wrong.

8

TRACES OF MY MOTHER
COLETTE

"**Y**ou did the right thing," Fintan tells me, though I can barely bring myself to care about his approval of my actions.

My eldest brother stands among the smattering of police officers, his light brown hair coiffed in the same style it's been since he was in high school. Short on the sides and back, two-inch swoop in the front.

"Good that you showed this to Dad. We need to move on this now."

My father's mouth has been in a tight line ever since I spun on my heel and marched right back into the salon to show him the note. I know for a fact that if we hadn't had our mini breakthrough, I would have hidden the threat on my life from him, afraid he would send me overseas again once he saw it.

To his credit, my father has been measured and on the job since his hot facial towel came off.

To my stylists' credit, the appointments haven't thinned out, even with the gaggle of squad cars in the parking lot of my business.

I am usually great at pretending. I can pretend I have a normal life expectancy. I can pretend I'm not in love with Rome. I can pretend all sorts of things with effortless grace. Pretending that it doesn't bother me to have a threat placed inside my locked car is no small feat, but my smile is up for the challenge.

Because I know the second Fintan or my father sees me panic, they will send me away again. So I march right back into my salon and sit a person waiting for a haircut into my chair on the end.

As I trim the woman's hair a quarter of an inch, I draw my calm from the extra dose of my medication and the fact that this madness will end with me. I will never have a daughter who will be haunted and hunted like I am.

When I feel the pinch of my genetics, it helps me to go to a file of saved photos on my phone and flip through until I feel grounded once more. If there is a picture of my mother on the internet, I have it in this collection. She received threats like this often, I've been told, yet in all the photos of her, she is poised and unbothered.

I want to be like that.

Once my client is finished, I steal the briefest of moments to glance at a photo of my mother in a deep blue gown, shaking hands with the Prime Minister, of all people.

She is beautiful and poised, as if no obstacle is too tall for her to cross over in her formidable heels.

I quickly tuck my phone in the pocket of my short sage pencil skirt, lest I appear unprofessional.

From the pictures I have seen of my mother, I am well aware that I set the tone for how worried other people allow themselves to be over these threats. Malice will always come; it always has come. But every picture I've seen of my mother in newspaper clippings features her with her chin held gloriously high, daring people to trifle her with anything other than her family, civil rights or fashion.

Mother was photographed to the hilt everywhere she went, so her favorite fashion designer sent her couture dresses for every event she attended. That was back when my parents did their part to push for peace between the races. My father stopped caring about most things once his wife died.

Maybe after Rome gets the West End under control, I can take up my mother's mantle and do my part to show the world that people who are different than us are still people worthy of protection, love and affection.

I swallow hard, ashamed that I am not doing all I can to help Rome and his people.

I got a few parks fixed up in the West End. That's all. I can do more than that. My mother would have done more.

Despite the fact that it is the middle of the day and there are cops and members of my family all over the place, the moment my client is finished with her new cut and style, I sneak into my office to call Rome.

He picks up on the second ring, which is very much his way. "What can I do for you, John?" comes his low, sexy voice.

I don't even mind that he calls me by a man's name. It's his way of telling me that he is not alone, but wishes he was, so he could seduce me nice and proper over the phone.

"I'm not doing enough," I tell him flat out. I don't have much time for niceties or the flirting I want to be doing.

I can picture Rome's frown. "I'm not sure what led you to that conclusion."

"My mother met with mayors and governors and prime ministers to push for vampire rights to be taken seriously. All I'm doing is cleaning up parks and opening a business that isn't segregated. I'm thinking too small."

I know Rome wants to voice his lengthy opinion on this, but because he is not alone, he can't. "I'm not sure what that would entail. It sounds like a lot of risk, and you already have your fair share of that."

I shrug, as if the whole thing is no big deal. "Then what's a little added danger? My mother had more risk aimed her way, and she still fought as long as her natural life would allow." I close my eyes, wishing for our beach, even though it's far too cold for that. Still, I would risk hypothermia for a sliver of clarity that comes from talking things through with someone who understands and loves me.

Before Rome can weigh in, I confess the thing I would normally keep to myself. My thoughts are all over the place, but I know before I end this call, I need to tell my boyfriend the most pressing item of the day. "I don't want a half relationship, where I assume you'll only want to be with me if I am strong and have everything in order."

"Absolutely. I'm glad you're telling me this."

I suck in a deep breath before the truth spills out. "I don't want you to worry, but I also don't want to hide things from you. Someone broke into my car this morning and left a note on my seat, threatening to abduct me if I didn't join the revolution and hand myself over."

There is a beat of silence, and then Rome springs into action. "Orlando, let's move. Nico, I need you to check on the Hillsbury account. Make sure no money moved that looks out of the ordinary."

I can hear Nico's surprise. "You're letting me look at accounts?"

"Can you handle it?"

I hear the wonder of Nino-bear's pride swelling at what

is clearly a promotion given to him from his big brother on the fly.

I'm guessing that wouldn't have happened if Rome didn't want his baby brother far away from the hint of our affair.

You're welcome, Nino-bear.

"Is the sheriff aware?" Rome asks me.

"Yeah. My father, Fintan and a few extra blues are at the salon. I'm not closing. I'm not affected," I lie. "It's all fine and under control. I just didn't want to hide it from you."

Rome's voice softens to a coo. I'm not sure how his sweetness could be disguised as being directed at "John". "I'm proud of you. That was the right thing to do. I'm on my way."

"Rome, it's okay. It's under control."

"But I'm not. I'm sure your people are just fine, but I won't sleep unless Orlando and I get a look at everything."

I blow a long breath out through pursed lips. "I didn't call to set off the alarms."

Rome chuckles. "Oh, trust me. This is me underreacting. You'll know if you've truly set off all my alarms."

I want to tell him I love him, but the knock on my door warns me our time is up. "You heard about this not from me, got it? Police scanner or whatever."

"Of course."

I end the call and then roll my shoulders back as I

move to open the door. Rachel's arms coil around my shoulders the second I emerge. "Tell me there's no reason to be afraid."

I squeeze her gently. "Of course not. My father comes by all the time, and it's no big deal."

"You know this is different. There are like, eight officers here." Her voice lowers. "I heard them, Colette. I heard what the note said."

Her fright does me no good, so I do my best not to feel it. I summon my mother's strength in my bones and don a confidence I wish was genuine. "Some people don't understand what we're doing here, but they will. They want our love to stay small and be directed only at humans, but that's not me, and I know that's not you."

Rachel sucks in a shuddering breath. "I knew the risks we were taking. But I don't think I fully understood the risks *you* are taking until now. They really broke into your car? In our parking lot?"

I kiss her cheek because I refuse to be anyone less than my perfect mother in this situation. "Everything is going to be okay." It's a promise Declan used to give me on the phone when we were so very far apart. It was a hollow promise, but I loved him for the lie. I needed to hear it, and I hope Rachel clings to it, too.

She nods and then releases me, turning to find my father watching us from a few feet away. "Sorry, Sheriff. You probably needed your daughter for something, and here I am, hogging her." She grins at my father, who surprisingly smiles at her.

My father extends his hand, shaking Rachel's grip with kindness in his eyes, in lieu of his usual stalwart nature. "Rachel, is it? I'm Elias. It's nice to meet you."

It shouldn't be strange to see my father being kind for no reason, but I can't look away from the oddity. The sheriff never wanted to meet my friends when I was little, other than to keep tabs on their parents. He was more concerned about the adults I might encounter. Besides, my best friend was Nino-bear, and we mainly kept to each other.

"Thanks for coming here, Sheriff. This whole thing has me a little on edge."

My father brings his other hand to rest atop their joined grip. "Don't you worry about a thing. We'll find out who did this. We always do."

That's a lie if I've ever heard one. We never do. We never get to the bottom of who sends me threatening letters. The only thing that made them stop the first time was when I moved away.

I don't know what to do with my dad when he takes an interest in my life or my friends that doesn't have anything to do with his job.

I shoot him a look of suspicion that says as much, but he pretends not to see it. "Nice girl, that one."

I nod, and then excuse myself, getting to my next client.

Dealing with threatening notes is one thing, but coming face to face with my father when he's being friendly? I still don't know how to do that gracefully.

I keep a chipper disposition about me and turn the volume up on the sultry singers of the jazz era, so no one feels the need to leave prematurely. Today is a normal, happy day. Nothing to see here.

That is, not until Rome and Orlando stalk in through the front door, garnering all eyes. Even the music seems to quiet in their presence.

Rome beelines for my father, motioning for a more private setting for their conversation.

I definitely don't want to be there for that.

I pretend my hardest, acting as if my heart doesn't long to swoon for Rome. I feign calm as if the threat doesn't affect me one bit.

My father, Fintan, Rome and Orlando head into my office, closing the door so they can work together to get to the bottom of this.

PIECING TOGETHER A PLAN
COLETTE

It's not twenty minutes before Fintan comes out and taps me on the shoulder, even though my hands are clearly busy cutting hair. "We need a word, Coco."

"Sure thing. I'll be finished in ten minutes." It should only take five to finish this client, but because Fintan didn't actually ask, but rather demanded, my fingers move slower out of spite.

Fintan is no stranger to my temperament, yet he still insists on bossing me around, rather than treating me like a person. "Fine. Hurry it up, though. This whole thing concerns you, you know."

"It does? Then it can wait until I have time to care about it."

Fintan chuckles, but it's a bitter sound. "You are such a brat."

"Leave me alone, or I'll shave your head. I have the power."

My client giggles. Even though Fintan is insufferable, many women turn into teenagers around him. They think he's good looking.

But then he opens his mouth. Not even the fact that we come from money can compensate for that.

After I finish up with my appointment, I help out by sweeping up, dawdling because it's my business, and I don't need to give the rebellion any credence by hurrying.

By the time I meander into my office, Fintan is positively stewing. "Took you long enough."

I respond by digging my pointy heel into the toe of his shoe on my way past him toward my desk. I sit in my seat, even though the four bulls are standing.

Just like that, I set the precedent that they don't control anything, least of all me. "How can I help you gentlemen?"

"This letter is concerning," the sheriff starts out. "But being that it's not the first, we need to move on this. It would be irresponsible not to."

Everything in me tightens, though I try not to let it show. "I am not moving out of Mayfield, if that's what you are suggesting."

I expect a fight from my father, but it's Fintan who speaks up. "You'll move where we put you, and you'll be grateful to be alive."

Orlando usually doesn't react to anything, but even he

can't remain stoic through Fintan's boorish nature. His raised eyebrows are louder than my brother's blustering. "That's what you want to tell the rebels? That we're afraid of a piece of paper? That a threat controls the Last Dead-blood, as well as the sheriff?"

Fintan scowls at Orlando. "What do you suggest, genius?"

Orlando's mouth firms, but he doesn't respond.

I place my hands flat on my desktop. "I suggest you start speaking like a boy who was raised with manners, Fintan. Our families are supposed to be working together, which you are making very difficult right now." I point to the Valentino enforcer. "Orlando is my big sweetie pie, so play nice."

Orlando narrows his eyes at my doting, but doesn't correct me.

Because he is my big sweetie pie.

My father nods in my direction. "You heard your sister. We come up with a plan together this time. Coco is part of this. She should have a say in our next move." Then he meets my eyes. "Not the only say, mind you, but a vote."

My heart swells that my father's words aren't just that. He's putting true action behind his promise that he won't be as controlling this time around.

Part of me that I didn't realize was suffocating begins to breathe for the first time. And in his presence, no less.

I guess miracles do happen.

Rome is uncommonly silent, which I know means he is freaking out on the inside.

The sheriff sets precedent by laying his cards out on the table, however bad his hand might be. "I think now is the time where we go through all our options. No bad ideas. We're not committing to anything. Everyone who wants a say gets one now."

"Declan," I remind them. "Declan is part of this. So is Nico."

Orlando nods, taking my suggestion as a directive. "I'll call them both now and fill them in."

Orlando doesn't leave the office, but speaks in low tones as he brings my brother and Rome's up to speed on the conversation via a three-way call.

"Why exactly is Nico being brought in on this?" Fintan complains, though his tone is slightly less hostile.

Rome doesn't respond, so my father jumps in. "Because an attack on Coco is a threat to all vampires. Rome looks out for his community, so his family deserves to be in on this. His people are the ones who will die if Coco is abducted again." The sheriff presses his pointer finger to the top of my desk. "We move as one family this time, like the old days."

Fintan grumbles in response.

I fight the urge to slug him.

"Nico is being brought in for the same reason Declan is being brought in on this," I reason. "We didn't use to act like two separate families. We used to be one family, Fintan. I want that again."

I keep my gaze from Rome because I know that if my father sees how I look at my secret boyfriend, he will know for certain that I am irreparably in love with this man.

Orlando finishes up his explanation on the three-way call to Nico and Declan, and then turns his phone on speaker, setting it atop my desk.

The sheriff takes the lead. "I'm not going to pretend I know what we should do, kids."

My heart warms because I know my father isn't just referring to Declan, Fintan and myself; he is including us all in the family, per my request.

The sheriff runs his hand over his face. "You know how we handled it the last time things got out of hand. We tracked down the bad guys as best we could, but they always were one step ahead of us. Coco was captured three times until I lost my temper with the whole thing and sent her away. Now here we are years later, and it's starting up again, so that method of sending her away didn't solve the problem; it only postponed it." He meets my eyes with actual openness. "I want all suggestions on the table. There's nothing in police training that covers any of this. We all know the stakes: Coco will be abducted, and her blood drained to try to exterminate an entire race of people. If anyone has an idea, speak up now."

I raise my hand. "Moving overseas isn't an option.

Mayfield will never change if we don't take a stand. We let the rebels chase me out of town last time, and things only grew worse."

Fintan crosses his arms, though not with excessive attitude. "I'm not sure that's the only factor, Coco. Halluci-blend running rampant is a major contributor to the divide in our city."

Fair point.

I'm still not moving.

The sheriff scratches at his chin. "I think video surveillance is a must around the salon and at your home."

My jaw firms. "Yes to the salon, but I need my home to be my home. I don't want surveillance there."

That would be the end of Rome's visits.

My father raises his hands. "No bad ideas in brainstorming. And I only meant for the outside perimeter, not the inside of your home."

I have no reason to refute this. No reason I can utter aloud, anyway. I don't want my father to see that Rome comes to my home. That would be a disaster. But I can't say this. His suggestion is perfectly reasonable.

I swallow hard.

Rome finally speaks up. "It's not enough. Until the threats go away, one of us needs to stay with her. She's fine at her salon. In the past, no one made a grab for her in public. These people thrive on anonymity. It's when she's on her own that she has been taken."

I don't like this sort of talk. I don't want a babysitter. I don't want my life discussed as if I am in constant danger. Yet I know the real issue is that it's not just me who is in danger, but the whole of the vampiric populace who will be in jeopardy if I am taken.

Nino-bear's exasperated sigh cuts through my armor. "Are you serious? Now we're protecting her?"

Orlando speaks in his cousin's defense. "It's not Colette we're defending, Nico; it's our people. If Coco is stolen and her blood used to make weapons, we all die. Think of it as protecting your own neck."

Fintan chimes in. "Seriously, Nico. If you don't think your people and your own lives are worth protecting, then that's good to know."

Nico gives a glum nonsensical reply, which I think means he's onboard. "It was easier when she just moved away. Is that really not on the table?"

It's a question I have wrestled with many times, but it still hurts when me leaving is seen as the only viable option.

My father runs his hand over his face, refusing to meet my gaze.

I clear my throat, feigning confidence I wish I felt. "Believe it or not, I am still abductable overseas. Radicals don't just stop their agenda because they might have to hop on a plane to do it."

Nico spouts back a catty, "Sure, but you're a sitting duck

here, smack in the middle of vampire territory. And if memory serves, you weren't snatched at overseas, only in Mayfield where things are most polarized."

I don't argue with Nico further. He has valid points, but that doesn't matter. I am not about to let a radical terrorist group come into my life and scare me out of my city. The Kennedys and the Valentinos helped build this city.

We also played a key part in destroying it.

Now it's time for me to help clean up the mess.

Declan's voice finally crackles from Orlando's phone. "Coco, are you alright? I don't care about any plans right now. Are you okay?"

Love for my brother fills my heart. It rarely matters how I feel about things. But my brother never forgets to remember me, even when I do.

"I have thoughts," I tell the room, but mostly I am speaking to Declan.

I can picture my brother's face. Declan is filled with understanding that is devoid of presumption. "I'm listening."

Those are the two most perfect words in the universe.

Though I haven't discussed this further with Rome, and haven't really delved in deeper with myself on the issue, I pull the trigger and speak my truth, however controversial.

"Hiding myself away didn't do anything to stop the

fighting between our races. The only thing that helped calm the tension was our mother."

Mom is a subject we don't talk about. Immediately, I feel my father and Fintan clamming up.

Fine by me.

"She used her unfortunate celebrity to show the world why the vampires deserve basic human rights. Because of her pushing so hard, they were able to own property outside of Mayfield. That wasn't a possibility before she involved herself."

Nico snorts, and before he even speaks, I know the next words that will come out of his mouth. "Yeah, that's a technicality they gave us with no intention of it helping us. They were counting on the people being so racist that even though we could own property, they knew no one would sell to us. Plus, banks wouldn't give vampires home loans, so it was a moot point. They gave us the ceremony of progress but kept us in place with their empty gift of nothing. And the second your mother died, they took even the charade of equality away, making it illegal to sell property to vampires outside of Mayfield."

Even though Nico can't see me, I hold up my hand to stop his legitimate tirade. "My mother did the heavy lifting and opened a lot of doors. Now it's my turn to make sure people can actually walk through them. She worked on policy; I want to work on the people. I can't do that while I'm hidden away."

Fintan gives my words a beat to sink in before he attempts to tear them apart. "How do you expect to do that? No one is listening."

I toss my hair over my shoulder, embracing the untouchable, entitled role I have been handed. "That's because the wrong people have been speaking. Newscasters report a disproportionate amount of crime coming from the West End of Mayfield, rather than showing human criminals. The wrong people are speaking when policies are not broken to give vampires more rights. Nico is absolutely right. Sure, they used to be able to own land outside of Mayfield, technically, and we patted ourselves on the back and called it a win. But no one would sell them a house outside of Mayfield. They are still banned from venturing into the East End. We've corralled them into one area and then cut off their resources so we can point at them and tell ourselves what a waste it is to invest in them."

Rome's chest puffs because I know he wants to say the same thing, but no one listens.

I can make people listen.

I tilt my head at my brother. "When was the last vampire wedding you went to, Fintan?"

My oldest brother opens and closes his mouth, but only incoherent spluttering comes out. "That's hardly fair," he manages. "Vampires can't legally get married."

I stand behind my desk, my palms kissing the top as I

let the piece of furniture bear my weight when I lean forward. "And we accept it. We give them one right, take it back, and withhold the others. Then we somehow expect them not to feel like the second-class citizens we have made them out to be. They can't even vote, Fintan. So who speaks for them? Who represents them when policies are made? It used to be our mother, but when she died, who took that role?"

Rome slides his sunglasses on to cover the raw emotion radiating out from him.

Of all people, Orlando is the one who answers my cry to the universe for justice. "No one," he says, his throat catching. "No one represents us. Before halluci-blend came to Mayfield, we were a nuisance. After halluci-blend infiltrated the West End, we became a danger. Now that they can't and won't help us clean up, there is no point in making new policies to help us; they want us gone. Gone or silent. Hence, the revolution wanting to steal you to end us."

I could say so many things in response to his truth, but instead of speaking, I move from behind my desk and beeline to Orlando. My knuckles brush against the locked door when I throw my arms around his towering form.

Orlando's entire body stiffens because he has no idea what to do with a hug from anyone other than Rome and Nico. "What are you doing?"

"I'm apologizing, which I can't very well do from across

the room. I didn't fight sooner. I expected other people to clean up the mess, to fight for your rights. I didn't stand up when I should have. I got your parks cleaned up and called it a day."

Orlando's rigid posture softens as he wraps one arm around my back. "You have your own problems to worry about. You're just trying to stay alive. It's not your fault the world is broken."

I look up at him, my eyes glassy with sincerity. "Yes, it is. My blood has killed countless vampires. The least I can do is make sure the ones who are left have a voice."

The room is silent, but for the pounding of my heart.

My big sweetie pie gazes at me with appreciation because in this moment, we are the same. We love Rome, and will do whatever it takes to make sure this life doesn't kill him.

Rome deserves better. They all do.

In a move uncharacteristic of the stoic Valentino enforcer, Orlando leans down and presses his lips to my forehead, sealing our connection as being that of family, and not obligation.

Orlando stands straighter and addresses my father. "I can watch her."

Fintan cocks his hip to the side. "What about Rome? Your whole job is to keep him safe. You can't be in two places at once."

Declan speaks up before I can open my mouth. "Rome,

can you do most of your work remotely? Because if you can, then you could stay at Coco's house with Orlando. He can watch you there."

My cheeks flush a fiery shade of pink. I worry it is obvious Orlando and Declan are pushing Rome and me together. If my father or Fintan find out...

My stomach twists with nerves.

Worst of all, what if Rome doesn't want to live with me? I know it's only temporary and circumstantial, but what if things are moving too fast for him?

Before I can figure out how to table this discussion until Rome and I can talk in private and make a decision we are both comfortable with, my secret boyfriend speaks up. "That's fine. When I have to go into the West End for my business, I'll make sure one of you three are with her. Otherwise, I'll sleep and do my remote work from Colette's house."

"You don't have to," I begin uncertainly.

Rome pulls out his cell phone to check a text, acting like this is all no big deal. "It's no trouble. I'll stay out of your hair, and Orlando will make sure no one snatches at you while you're in your home. We can get you to and from the salon, too. Does your place have a spare bedroom?"

"Yes, but..."

"And you live in Midtown now, right?"

"Yes."

He puts his phone away and motions in my direction.

"Your mother was a force to be reckoned with. It is no surprise you're turning out the same way. Whatever support you need from our family, you have it. I agree that hiding you away won't stop the revolution. Best take a stand now. We'll be there to take the bullets aimed your way."

A thrill of emotions runs through me, but before I can dissect all the moving parts, I turn to my father. "Sheriff, I think it's time I do more than just intimidate the mayor. If we're going to push for policy changes, we need him on our side for more than just posterity's sake. I need a meeting with him. Can you make that happen?"

My father's chin lifts. I can tell he is readying himself for the dawning of a new era. "Whatever you need, I'm here."

Rome lifts his finger. "I'd like to sit in on that meeting."

The sheriff nods. "I'll take care of it."

And just like that, the Valentinos and the Kennedys have a plan to change the world.

PLANNING A BETTER WORLD
COLETTE

Orlando wasted no time at all converting my office into a second bedroom. My futon was replaced with a more comfortable sleeper sofa so it could pull out to suit whomever was on the schedule for guarding me that day. Plus, there is a standard bed in the room, in case more than just Orlando winds up staying the night.

"Is it fair to say that I really hate this, but I'm also really grateful?" I ask Declan as I pack up my purse for the morning.

Declan sips his coffee at my kitchen counter. "It's only fair if I get to say that I'm proud of you." He sets his mug down, keeping his eyes from mine. "Are you ready for the meeting with the mayor today?"

I shrug. "The mayor is small potatoes. What's he going to say? That he's happy about all the violence? That he loves giving tax breaks to any human willing to move to

Mayfield? I have a feeling that we're closer to being on the same page than we are farther apart on the issues."

Declan shakes his head. "That's the thing, though, isn't it. Our list of issues is different than the mayor's. He wants the East End to thrive and to take credit for it all. You want actual love and acceptance for everyone."

I consider my brother's wisdom but shrug it off soon after. "Meh. It'll lead us to the same place, which is to get Mayfield back on steadier feet. The mayor's ego will drag him along for the ride, just like it did when I strong-armed him into funding the cleanup of the West End parks."

Declan taps his finger to the countertop. "Mom would have had a plan. A list of topics to tackle. This isn't about making friends, Coco. If you want to make changes, you need to be specific about them. Line them up like dominoes so you don't knock the wrong one over first. Otherwise, we'll make a bigger mess of things than already exists. If you don't lay out a clear plan with expectations, then we're all just shaking hands and smiling for the cameras, which has been done to death."

I blanch at the mental image. "Gross. I don't want to do that." I fish around in my purse for my pad of paper, pulling it out with great hesitance. "I have a list, Declan, but I'm not sure the mayor will want to hear it."

Declan takes the notebook I offer to him and flips to the first page. Though his lips turn to a frown, I know that's just how his face looks when he is concentrating.

At least, I hope that's all it means.

When the seconds of silence begin to pile up, I backpedal. "I'm not going to actually bring any of this up with the mayor today. It's just some thoughts I've put together over the last few months. It's my guess of what might help Mayfield, but I don't know. Maybe it will make it all worse."

Declan flips to the next page, his eyes widening. "You're pushing for public school reform? For budget reallocation? They're not going to like this."

I bristle. "Well, if I was a vampire mother, I wouldn't like sending my child to a school that is vastly underfunded."

Of course, I will never be a mother or a vampire, so I can only imagine their pain.

Declan taps the paper. "This is a lot, Coco."

I cave at the first sign of opposition, which isn't a good sign. "I'm just going to shake the mayor's hand and let him know I'm pushing for peace. That's all. It's a photo op to send a message to whomever is leaving these threats for me, so they see I'm not going to hide again, nor am I going to join their revolution."

Declan still doesn't respond, other than to take a pen out of his pocket and scribble a note next to one of mine. "This is good, Coco. This is real good. I'm just adding a few clarifying points you might want to mention when you bring these up to the mayor."

My eyes widen. "*When* I bring it up? You really think I should push for policy change right off the bat?"

Declan shrugs. "I think he's been in office for years, yet he hasn't tried to do any of this. If you don't push him, I'm not sure anyone will." His eyes widen when he hits the page for the school's budgets, noting how underfunded the West End schools are compared to the East End. "Are these numbers accurate?"

"Accurate and horrible, yes. I've been doing my research. Didn't want to go into this blind."

Declan nods. "Well done."

I gnaw on my lower lip, considering how badly this meeting might go if I push for the big changes instead of smiling my way toward small alterations of convenience.

One thought keeps coming back to me. "I don't want more small changes that affect nothing. Peace is possible, but this city has to break before it can be properly rebuilt."

Declan slides the notebook back to me. "I think we've been patient long enough." Declan stands, finishing up his coffee and sliding his jacket on. "One of us should be able to get married. If it's not me, then I want it to be you."

I nearly choke on the air in my lungs. "What?" I blink at him and then back up, setting my purse down to let him know we are talking about this. He can't just drop a conversational bomb like that and leave. "I'm not marrying anyone. You know that. I'm in love with Rome, who can't legally get married to anyone." I pinch the bridge of my nose. "And even if I could marry him, I wouldn't."

Declan snorts his disbelief. "Right."

"I wouldn't. I'm not about to marry someone I'll make a widower a year or two later."

Declan stiffens, his mouth tightening because we don't often talk about my inevitable decline. "Don't talk like that. You know I hate it."

"Then don't assume I want something I can't want."

Declan zips up his jacket. "For the record, I was talking about me being bummed that I can't get married without coming out to the family and watching them implode. That was my way of telling you I met someone."

My mouth falls open as shock and awe flood my system. Before I can stop myself, my arms throw themselves around my brother's neck. "You met someone?! Tell me everything! Who is he? What does he like to do? How did you meet? When do I get to meet him?"

A small smile teases Declan's mouth. His neck shrinks as I step back to get a look at what my brother is like when he's in love. "His name is Lucas. He's funny and considerate. He likes baseball, and even though it's the most shamefully boring sport in the world, he makes it fun."

Declan's cheeks are pink. I can't believe I never realized he was seeing someone.

"How long have you two been sneaking around together?"

"Four months, but we've known each other longer than that. It just sort of turned into something more and we're going with it."

My mouth falls open. "Four months?! That's a long time to keep something as huge as an entire relationship from your favorite sister."

Declan quirks his brow at me, silently telling me that I am guilty of the exact same thing.

I cross my arms in a huff. "Oh, fine. Still, I'm offended. I want to know these things."

Declan leans back. "I know it hasn't been all that long, but I'm telling you, I have never felt like this before. I can't speak for him, but I'm done looking. Lucas is it for me."

I don't hold back my swoon. My hand rests over my heart while images of my brother being happy with his special fella wash over me. "Declan, that is amazing. I'm meeting him tomorrow night."

Declan's eyes widen. "Are you serious? I'm not... Dad can't..."

I grip my brother's wrist. "I know the rules. You don't want the sheriff and Fintan to know you're gay. You know I'm not going to push you on that. But you also know that you and I aren't meant to keep secrets. It killed me to keep Rome from you."

Declan grumbles under his breath. "Yes, well my secret isn't nearly as damning as yours."

"Exactly. So you and Lucas can come over tomorrow night for dinner. It's perfect."

I fight the urge to ask all the questions that Declan no doubt doesn't want to think about.

When my brother still looks uncertain about letting his two worlds meet, I put my hand on my hip. "He should meet your family, Declan. If you love this guy, I want to know him."

Declan purses his lips and then exhales. "Fine, but only you. You know how Dad and Fintan are."

I don't love it that Declan and I need to have our own separate family apart from our father and Fintan, but I loathe more the idea that Declan felt he couldn't tell me about his special guy.

"What if you don't like him?" Declan voices one of his many insecurities as he helps me with my coat.

I chortle at his query. "Do you love Rome?"

Declan shrugs. "He's growing on me."

That comes as a surprise to me. "Well, I'm glad to hear that. Your guy could have a fifth limb and hate puppies, and I'd still love him. I'm so happy for you, Declan."

My brother opens the door for me while I fetch my purse and flit into the garage.

I don't drive my car much anymore. Whoever is staying with me that night is in charge of getting me where I need to go, and taking me home.

No one can leave a note in my car if I don't have one

parked at the salon, after all. I don't love being totally dependent on the men in my life, but I know that if the situation was reversed and it was Declan who needed protection, pride would not be a logical reason to risk his life.

I need to live long enough to change the way the world views vampires.

Declan starts up his car while my fingers run over my notebook in my purse.

I have never spoken my ideas aloud, but when I meet with the mayor today, everything in my notebook will be laid out in the open for the winds of change to blow them into the future, where hopefully they belong.

11

FIVE MINUTES
COLETTE

I took my pill this morning, but my hands are beginning to tremble. If I am going to start having more and more of these meetings that my mother used to go on, I might need to make my peace with taking two doses a day on the regular.

I hate being dependent on drugs like this. But I guess I hate not being in control of my body even more.

My father sits on one side of me in the city hall reception area while Rome is on my other, though he has left an empty chair between us for propriety's sake.

Orlando stands at the exit. He is my silent gargoyle who has no personality that is carelessly left visible to the public.

I fight the urge to make Orlando sit down beside me. He can't be comfortable, standing at attention like that all the livelong day.

Rome checks his cell phone. "The mayor is five minutes late." He stands, his expression stony. "Let's go, Orlando."

I stand, confused at Rome's small waves of anger. "The mayor's probably just running late, is all. He'll come."

I could just barge in, like I did the last time when I was amped up about the state of the parks in the West End, but this time, I want an actual meeting where we are on the same team.

That's the hope, anyway.

Rome's expression softens, but it's not affection he sends my way. I see only pity in his eyes, as if I have yet to understand the ways of the world. "He's not going to meet with you if we're here, Coletta."

My eyes widen at his slip. He only calls me that when we're alone.

Luckily, the notion of a vampire being affectionate to a human is about as foreign to my father as an alien invasion, so the blunder goes unnoticed.

I frown at Rome. "I don't think that's what's happening here. It's only been five minutes."

"And my time is worth more than what he'll belittle it to become."

My father doesn't argue with Rome, but stands and shakes his hand. "Once we get inside, I'll text you." He motions to the front desk where the man taking phone calls has yet to look our way. "If you have trouble getting through reception, I'll come out and escort you in."

I can tell this hurts Rome's pride, but he nods. "That works."

"I'm sure Mayor Stapleton is just running late," I argue.

Rome moves toward the exit of the waiting room. "*I'm* sure that a minute after I leave, the mayor will magically become available."

I look not to my dad and not to Rome, but to Orlando for the real story. "Is that true?"

Orlando's jaw is tight. "Always has been, always will be. We're here because *you* believe the world can change, Coco, not because *we* believe it."

My heart sinks. Maybe this should be more of a meet and greet to get us at least on friendly terms, since that is clearly not the base on which we are starting.

The two exit while the sheriff and I sit back down. "This was a bad idea," I worry aloud.

My father sits back without letting the room around him affect his stoic mood. "That never stopped your mother. I highly doubt it'll stop you. That's the thing about you reckless Kennedy women. Even if it's a bad idea, a dangerous one, a deadly one—the Kennedy women will act with such finesse and confidence that you'll swear it was the right move all along."

I marvel up at him. "You really think that about me?"

He motions out with his hands. "I'm here, aren't I?"

I mull over his words, testing them for lies. "Thank you. Thank you for being here. Even if nothing changes, I need to try."

And that's when it dawns on me that I truly do need to give this an honest try, even if the wall between reason and bigotry is steeper than I realized.

I have to try.

Sure enough, not a minute after Rome and Orlando exit, the mayor's secretary looks up at us. "Mayor Stapleton will see you now."

My jaw ticks with a ripple of anger.

Oh, will he? Now that there aren't any vampires, he'll see me?

I stand with renewed purpose, not bothering to quell the fire in my soul. I shift from nervous lamb to prowling lion, ready to devour my prey.

I stalk into the mayor's office, ready to speak until I am heard.

12

MEETING WITH THE MAYOR
COLETTE

I don't shake the mayor's hand, not because I want to start a fight right off the bat, but because I am not going to let anyone see my fingers trembling this early in the game. Instead of a handshake, I feign that we are the sort of people who will get along instantly, so I go in for a kiss on the cheek. "It's good to see you, Mayor Stapleton. Thank you for making the time to meet with us."

Mayor Stapleton is sweatier in person than he is on television. His rounded belly is smoothed out by well-fitted clothes, but it is clear from his eyes darting toward the closed door that he has been dreading this meeting.

I will my hands to settle, telling my body that we now have the upper hand, so there is no need to be on edge.

"Have a seat. Sheriff, Miss Kennedy."

"Madam Deadblood," I correct him, choosing the most formidable name the media has given me.

There are two chairs opposite his desk, which tells me he had no intention of letting Rome and Orlando inside. Yet he won't go so far as to refuse to meet with them, because that would be bad for his image.

What a weasel.

Before I can start with my prepared speech, the mayor and my father start joking around. They talk about the weather, of all things. Then they discuss the bang-up job they've done in keeping the East End's crime rate down for so long.

Letting off the junkies in the East End by taking them to rehab is how my father has kept the crime rate in the East End down, while it's been assumed the crime is out of control in the West End because the vampires aren't given an option for rehab, but are carted right off to jail.

About ten minutes in, I turn to my father. "Don't you have a phone call?"

The sheriff grimaces and then ducks his head. "Excuse me, Jim. I'll be right back. My daughter has a few things she would like to discuss."

My frustration over being ignored doesn't affect my tone, but it does increase how direct I am willing to be. Before the mayor can work out a pacifying comment, I cross one leg over the other, leaning back in my seat. "Now that you two finished patting yourselves on the back for a job half-done, perhaps we can discuss allocating funds to help revive the West End."

The mayor's mouth falls open. "I'm sorry? *More* funds than what I just doled out to clean up the parks over there?"

"Far more, in fact. The funds aren't being distributed evenly throughout Mayfield."

"And how do you guess that?"

I fix him with a simpering expression. "By the magic of sight. Most of the publicly owned property landscaping is handled by landlords in the West End, as opposed to the city, because the city doesn't lift a finger to do the same job it does in the East End over there for them." I hit my next point, knowing there's no turning back now. "The vampire school is so underfunded, the children are sharing textbooks, while the children in the East End have multiple digital devices assigned to each student. I want to know where the vampire tax money is going, since it is clearly not being spent on them."

My father comes back inside with an apologetic smile on his face and Rome and Orlando in tow. "See, Mister Valentino? The mayor wasn't dodging you. He was right here the whole time."

The mayor's secretary comes in behind the three. "I'm sorry! Mayor Stapleton, they just stormed right past me."

Orlando stares him down. "We had an appointment."

"But you can't possibly think..."

Rome takes the seat beside me—my father's seat—setting the tone of importance to which the room will be expected to follow.

I love it.

If we were alone, oh, the filthy things I would do to this man on this very desk.

The sheriff pats the secretary on the back good naturedly. "Don't worry. I'll call the cops to make sure no other vampires show up for the appointments they book in broad daylight. The nerve."

I snicker under my breath. I didn't know my father could be funny.

Mayor Stapleton stands, smoothing the buttons on his dull blue dress shirt as his forehead dampens anew. "Mister Valentino, I wasn't expecting..."

Rome's cool yet authoritative demeanor is a stunning sight, indeed. "You weren't expecting me to show up to my appointment with you? How shameful of me to tolerate a reputation where people don't take my word seriously. Tell me, are you in the habit of making an old man stand? Because there are only two chairs here, and nothing for the sheriff."

The mayor motions for the secretary to grab two more chairs, though I know Orlando won't deign to sit in one. "My oversight. What can I do for you today, Mister Valentino?"

I lean forward. "I believe Mister Valentino might

prefer you answer my question before dodging the subject. Why is it that appropriate, equal funds have not been allocated to the West End? Their population is denser than the East End, yet they are underfunded two to one."

Rome sits back in his seat, relaxing while Mayor Stapleton squirms. "I was thinking this was more a favor to your father, meeting you."

I pull authority out of my hat and wave it around as if I know what I'm doing with it. "And I was thinking you were serious about taking this meeting. I have an appointment with the governor tomorrow, and I'd like to be able to give her some answers."

If that's not a bluff, I don't know what is.

Luckily, no one gives me away.

The mayor leans forward, looking like he has finally caught on to the fact that he is on the job. "You have a meeting with the governor about this? I can't imagine she has opinions on how the budget of Mayfield has been divided up."

I let out a light laugh that has bitter notes ringing through it. "Funny, that. See, it turns out that everyone cares when whole chunks of our society are ignored, yet taxed as if they matter equally with the others. With the crime rate being what it is, Mayfield is getting all the wrong sort of notoriety. Why wouldn't the governor care about that?"

The mayor opens and closes his mouth. "What you're asking isn't something you can demand."

His dodge does nothing to cool my temperament.

Declan was right. Playing nice and making friends won't do a darn thing. You can't change what hasn't been brought to light.

"Believe it or not, I am capable of doing the barest amount of research. I am so amazing that I can call the school board of a high school in the East End and ask them for a copy of their public numbers, and then I can call the school board in the West End, too." I fix the mayor with a cool smile. "I know, color me impressed with myself. Two phone calls in one day. And I managed to file my nails."

When it's clear to my father that he is part of a meeting that has gone further south than he was prepared for, he dips his head to the room. "I've got some work to see to. Let me know if my daughter makes the mayor cry, will you, Orlando?"

"Give her five minutes, Sheriff." Orlando slaps my father's hand just before my father exits.

If that isn't the cutest thing...

Now the gloves can really come off.

I take a gold pen off the mayor's desk just to be a brat and dominate his space. I tear off a piece of my notebook paper, promising myself I will not leave this room until actual change is in the works.

"Being that there are more vampire children in Mayfield than human children, their school should have more funding."

The mayor shakes his head. "That's not how this works. Funding isn't per capita; it is allocated based on test scores. The West End scores lower every year, so they get less funding."

Rome's jaw tightens, so I double down on my directness. "Let me get this straight: underfunded schools have children who score lower? And every year, the gap gets wider and wider, until they are considered lucky if they graduate at all? I certainly hope you are merely stupid and not diabolical. We can work with stupid, but corruption runs deep."

Rome angles his torso toward me. "If the stain is too deep, then sometimes it's not worth it to try to make it better." His eyes narrow in on the mayor. "Sometimes it's more advantageous to throw out the trash and start fresh with someone else."

The mayor draws himself up. "Is that a threat? Are you threatening me?"

Rome tilts his head to the side. "Are you a stain on society? You heard Madam Deadblood's question: are you stupid or are you racist? Can you improve or are you unfit for your post?"

I lean forward. "Your post is to represent both ends of your city, not just the people who look and act like you."

"I was elected by votes from the East End," the mayor argues. Though, as his words hit the air, I can tell he regrets them.

My words come out slow and deadly. "Could that be because vampires don't have the legal right to vote?"

And just like that, the mayor's mouth snaps shut.

"Here is what I want this month," I begin, sitting back in my seat to mirror Rome's feigned ease. "I want a meeting with you and the person who does the budget for the city. I want this meeting tomorrow at nine in the morning. Dirty stains on society are easier to spot in the daylight, don't you think, Rome?"

My boyfriend casts me a sliver of a smile. "That's the rumor. I just so happen to be available tomorrow morning. Do you think the reporters who follow you around like lost puppies might be up and ready for a story by then?"

I feign a gasp of awe and touch my sternum. "I daresay they might. Fantastic idea."

"Tomorrow is a weekend," the mayor reminds me, earning a well-timed glare from Rome and myself.

Rome's voice is controlled without a hint of hurry. "I believe you've wasted enough weekends to spare us one. If the Last Deadblood is requesting a meeting, you can either comply, or I can *make* you comply. Then again, perhaps the media can guilt you into caring about the people you are supposed to represent. Either way, you will be where Madam Deadblood wants you."

The mayor's blustering is expected, but largely ineffectual.

"Tomorrow morning, I will be here to meet with you and your budget person," I continue, grateful Rome is beside me. "We will make some much-needed changes so that the children of the West End have a chance. I am ashamed that you've lost faith in a people you were elected to protect. This is their only safe place in the world, and you've made them fight for every scrap of respect and opportunity."

The mayor's face is red. "Young lady, I do not appreciate being lectured."

I do my best to remain unruffled, though I have to say, being called "young lady" irks me. "I don't much care what you appreciate. I don't appreciate you dropping the ball so badly that I have to come in and teach you how to stand up straight. You time in the sun is over, old man."

That's right. A "young lady" deserves an "old man."

The mayor loosens his collar. "What makes you think you can come in here and demand anything?"

I stand, deeming the meeting as over. I got what I wanted: a meeting with someone who can change policies.

Still, I stare down the mayor as Rome rises beside me. "I can demand citizens are treated fairly because I live in this city. I can demand meeting after meeting because there is no shortage of people who want to gawk at the Last Deadblood. It seems my curse comes with a few perks, and it's high time I tapped into them to incite a bit of change." I go for the bare truth, even if it makes me squirm on the inside. "I opened a business in Midtown, and suddenly, commerce in that area is booming. I breathed life into that neighborhood simply by going there." I look him up and down, owning every bit of my privilege to the hilt. "I want to use my power to help Mayfield. You've been using your power to help only the people who are like you. You had your chance to do the right thing. Now I'm going over your head. Either get on board or watch your career slip through your fingers. I don't care which you choose; change is happening now. Take credit or take the blame. Those are your only choices."

Rome pauses at the door Orlando opens for us. He turns his chin over his shoulder to fix the mayor with a calculating stare. "We will see you here at nine tomorrow. Call in anyone you need to make the changes Madam Deadblood demands. Patience is a virtue I've never put much stock in. Do not test my temper on this."

A thrill runs through my spine as we exit. Though my hands are trembling, my heels are steady as we make our way to the street.

"That was incredible," Rome says in a quiet whisper meant only for me. "You are a sight, tré-sur. Tell me I am on the schedule tonight to stay with you."

I grant him a small smile. "Absolutely. Wear exactly

this outfit and exactly that adoring expression." It's a good joke, because he only wears the one thing: black fitted slacks and a white dress shirt with the cuffs rolled, paired with a silver belt buckle.

Rome brushes my hip covertly. "I don't know any other kind of expression to wear when I look at you."

Orlando opens the back door of the tinted window sedan for me.

Before I slide in, I tilt my head up at the autumn sky, embracing every bit of the sunshine in Mayfield.

Maybe there is hope for this divided city after all.

13

PLANS AND CONFESSIONS
COLETTE

Rome, Orlando and I stayed up half the night drawing up different plans and figures based on the misappropriated school budget. We don't hesitate to pull out all the stops, tapping into our resources to make sure the meeting is set up to play in our favor.

I took a leap yesterday and actually got through to the governor, requesting her presence at the meeting today. Only because I am the Last Deadblood was I able to get through, combined with my father's position in the city.

Rome sips his espresso at the dining table while I recline against his chest in my chair beside his, munching on a piece of toast. He kisses my shoulder. "Did I tell you that I'm impressed with you? I can't believe all you've accomplished in such a short time."

"I've been so focused on my curse being a curse that I forgot about the perks. Telling the mayor that I had the governor's ear was a bluff, but after I said it, I knew I would have to make it true." I recall my fruitful conversation with the governor yesterday over the phone. "She didn't need as much strong-arming as she did sweet talking, thank goodness. It's exhausting being intimidating. I don't know how you keep it up."

My cheek presses to Rome's. It's like I can't get close enough.

I fell asleep on the couch last night after a fair few hours spent discussing the future of Mayfield. Rome carried me to bed, but slept on the floor until I roused at four in the morning and nearly stepped on his stomach on the way to the bathroom.

"What are you doing on the floor?" I asked him, groggy and sleepy-eyed.

"I didn't want to be away from you," he admitted, sitting up. "Is that okay?"

I pulled him up, kissing his lips that were puffy from sleep. "You don't sleep on the floor, sweetheart. Come and sleep in my bed with me."

Rome's kiss deepened, expressing gratitude and loyalty without words.

When I came back from the bathroom, I curled up beside him, reveling in the feel of his chest pressed to my spine and his arm heavy across my middle.

To wake up like that was divine. Aside from my shower, we've been inseparable ever since.

Orlando sips his coffee while making phone calls to set up his day. He hasn't said much, but I can tell the added meeting is setting them back on whatever skull-cracking they had on their docket for the day.

"I'm sorry I'm taking you both away from your normal workdays," I offer.

Orlando pauses between phone calls to respond. "These meetings will make our future workdays easier, so you don't have to worry about putting us out. This is important, Coco. Make sure you're on your game today. Did you take your meds?"

I sour whenever anyone asks me that. Though, being that I tried unsuccessfully to wean myself off them not too long ago, I understand I've earned the hovering.

Plus, I can't be mad at my big sweetie pie. He's such a grumpy little love bug.

"I haven't yet, but I will before we go."

Truthfully, this morning I am far steadier than I expected to be. No part of me is trembling, and there's no loss of control in sight. Even though I am nervous about the meeting today, my body isn't feeling the effects of my anxiety.

Still, I know better than to go off my meds again. If nothing else, I might not have to take two pills today, which is a victory.

I finish off my toast. "I can't believe the governor is

actually coming today. It was such a long shot that I would actually get through."

Rome kisses my shoulder. "You're used to being hidden away. Your mother understood her power and used it to help our kind. You're just coming into your birthright." He kisses my cheek. "I'm glad I get front row seats. Nowhere I'd rather be."

Orlando sets his phone down. "I need to use your printer, Coco. We need hard copies of this plan to pass out to everyone there. We can't chance a miscommunication, and I don't want them to rush us through our points just to get rid of us."

"Of course. It's in the office. Or, what's now your bedroom. It's tucked in the closet."

The moment Orlando exits, Rome traces his fingers down my silhouette. He buries his nose in the crook of my neck, inhaling deeply. "I was thinking of asking Declan if I can switch with him tonight. I know it's his night to stay here, but as often as I can, I want to wake up with you in my arms. That was perfection."

"Mm." I revel in the feel of his addiction to my skin. My hand reaches up to bunch in his thick obsidian hair. "Not tonight. Declan and I have plans. But any day after today, yes."

"You two going to the movies?"

"No. I'm meeting his secret person. It's only fair; he met mine."

Rome chuckles. "I didn't know Declan had a secret girl-friend. Is she as controversial as you dating me? I can't imagine what reason he might have to keep her a secret."

I bite my tongue to keep from outing my brother to my boyfriend.

Rome sips his espresso, seeming just as content as I am to be this close doing such a normal thing. "Are you happy that you can lean on Rachel? Is she a solid branch manager?"

"She's fantastic. The hesitation in stepping back was all my own hang-ups. I hate taking my hands off a project, but it was time. If I'm going to be doing more things like this to help the West End, I need someone to run the salon." I sigh wistfully. "If only I could clone myself. Then I could be in two places at once and I wouldn't have to delegate."

His lips trail up the slope of my neck. "Ah, but dele-gating is one of the calling cards of a successful business. You'll just have to make your peace with the fact that your business is thriving because you built something that can last even if you close your eyes at night." He removes his lips from my neck to finish his cup. "Or, you know, while you start a revolution with the dregs of society."

I know he's kidding, but I don't like it. "You are not the dregs of society. You are working to clean up a mess that has taken years to create. By the time we are done with the West End, it will be the most thriving piece of land in the nation."

"Only the nation?" Rome sniffs. "I was thinking of being the best in the world."

"As you wish it, darling."

Rome chuckles low and deep as he turns me slightly so he can kiss me without holding back.

His fingers trail down my cheek as his breath fans my face. "If I asked you for something, would you consider it?"

I cannot imagine what he could possibly want that I might hold back from him. "Of course."

Another kiss. Another thumbing of my cheek.

"I want a drawer here. Somewhere I can keep a change of clothes, so I feel like I live here with you. Since Orlando and I are on the roster to watch your house, it wouldn't be too suspect if your family found them, I don't think."

My mouth falls open at the very normal thing a boyfriend might want that I never even considered.

A few months. We've been dating only a handful of months. Alarm bells should be ringing that this is happening too fast, but there is only the quietness of peace that engulfs me when I reply with a tender, "I'll clear out a drawer for you tonight."

His shoulders deflate as a satisfied smile sweeps over his features. "I know it's soon. Truthfully, I've never asked a woman that before. But when I'm with you, I don't want to leave."

The wish for him to move in with me nearly touches

my tongue, but the second I consider voicing those words, reality falls on my shoulders.

We can never live together, unless we come clean to my father and the world. If that ever happened, our relationship wouldn't be about us anymore; it would be about everyone else.

I don't want that.

I clear my throat. "I'll order a nightstand for Orlando to keep his things in for his overnights, too, so it isn't suspect if Fintan finds your clothes here."

I stand from the table and take my dish to the sink, envisioning the protests and jeers that would be hurled at us if we dared be together in public. Will we ever be able to walk down the street holding hands? Is there any chance of normalcy?

I wash the morning dishes, my mind plagued with the damning notion that this is the most Rome and I will ever have: a drawer and a good excuse to see each other with no one suspecting a thing.

My heart is heavy now as the three of us discuss in detail the topics we are going to broach today. Even when the governor's assistant calls to ask if they can invite a member of the press into the meeting, I'm still not feeling much optimism or cheer.

Orlando shuts the notebook where we've been taking notes. "I think we're prepared. Whatever they argue can't possibly hold weight against all this." He taps his finger to the closed notebook. "We should get going. I don't want to be the last ones there."

I stand and reach for my cell phone. "I just need to make a quick call to Declan, and I'm ready."

I move down the hall with cement in my soul. I wish the world could be different, or that it somehow had a place for Rome and me.

Though I don't wish the burden of my secret relationship on anybody, I am grateful it was Declan who discovered us. It means I have someone to talk to when things start to feel too complex to puzzle through alone.

My brother's voice is chipper as I shut myself in my bedroom. "Everything okay? You caught me on my lunch break. Good timing, Coco."

"Everything's great," I reply with such glumness that it almost sounds bitter. "I'm in a relationship with a man I adore. Rome asked for a drawer to put his clothes in at my house. I couldn't feel closer to a man than I do him."

"Well don't sound too cheerful about it. Those sound like good things, kiddo. Fast, but good."

"It's both fast and good, but it's also all it can ever be. We can't go on a date. He can't meet my family as my boyfriend, other than you. We can't hold hands in public. We can't..." I hold in my sweeping depression, willing it to pass by quick and leave me unscathed. "We can't build a life together unless it's covered up."

Declan doesn't shine a new light on the conundrum.

This grim reality is all there is. "That sounds hard. Is this what you want? Because those are not small things you're giving up." He takes in a deep breath and lowers his voice so as not to be overheard. "Not that my situation is the same, but it's similar enough that I have to ask myself those same things. In the end, I decided Lucas is worth taking a chance on, even if it breaks my heart that it can't be out in the open."

I bite my tongue, wanting to argue that he absolutely could have a relationship with this man out in the open. He might lose the sheriff and Fintan over it, but he could publicly date Lucas. He could live with him without a cover story.

I can't do any of those things.

"The world will never be okay with us," I say aloud, my words leaving a hollow feeling in my stomach. "I love Rome, and I have to pretend he means nothing to me. Can I keep this up forever?"

"Only you can answer that."

Darn Declan for never telling me what to do. He's the only person who I wish would overstep.

Declan's voice is quieter now. "Is Rome worth it?"

"Yes." My reply comes quick and without hesitation. "It just feels heavy. You'll never get drunk at my wedding, Declan."

The silence gives us both a hug when I need it most. My brother is careful with my melancholy. "Then we'll get drunk tonight. Who knows? Maybe one day, Lucas and I will be so in sync that the four of us can double date. No one would suspect you're with a vampire."

"But I don't want a secret life. I want to dress Rome up in pretty suits and parade him around the city. I want to feed him pasta and blush when he kisses my cheek at a restaurant."

Declan is my best friend for many reasons—one of those being that he doesn't try to cheer me up out of turn. "I'm sorry, Coco. You're right. You'll never have that with Rome. I'm no relationship expert, but you should probably tell him how you feel."

I groan. "Can you imagine? We're a few months in, and you expect me to bring up the fact that I'm pouting because we can't get married? The whole thing would be moot because he would run away faster than I could finish the sentence. No, no. It's fine. It's just dawning on me that a drawer might be the closest we'll ever get to long-term bliss."

"And you're already there. This is a happy day, Coco. Maybe we can feel sad about it in half a year when you two are having those sorts of discussions organically."

"Yeah. You're right. Are we still on for tonight?"

"Unless I get cold feet and back out, which is a likely possibility. If you don't like Lucas, I'm going to bum real hard."

I scoff. "I already know I'm going to love Lucas. I'll make him my new favorite brother."

"Hey! What about Fintan? You know, he was just at his buddy's warehouse in Dazier for their regular poker game. Maybe he won you something shiny."

"Doubtful." Finally, I manage a smile. "I'll call you when we're done with our meeting. Wish me luck?"

"Break their kneecaps."

It's our version of "break a leg."

When I end the call, loneliness taps me on the shoulder, though I know it shouldn't. It felt so good to have Rome sleeping beside me last night. His body curved around mine as if we were twin sculptures carved from the same stone.

A long breath drags in and out of me as I remind myself that this is not a solvable problem—not today, at least.

Today I am going to deal only with the budget for the school system of Mayfield. Nothing else is going to steal my focus.

At least, that's what I tell myself.

When I open the door, I come face to face with none other than Rome. "Oh! Hi, I was just chatting with Declan."

Rome looks spooked and mildly breathless. "I was eavesdropping." His eyes are wide with the confession that spills out of him like vomit. "I don't think I meant to. I was picking up the copies Orlando printed off and I heard my name. Then I was eavesdropping on purpose."

I hem and haw and do my best to backpedal, but I'm not sure I am all that coherent. "I didn't mean... You didn't hear me correctly." My fist rests on my hip as I frown up at him. "I'm not sure what you heard."

"You want to be with me in public. You want to marry me. You said that you love me, and our love makes you sad sometimes because it has to be secret."

My nape dampens with sweat. "I don't... It's not what I meant."

This is it. This is the moment he pulls away. I can feel him leaving without looking back at the carnage that is my ruined heart if he goes.

I brace myself and hold my breath as I wait for his inevitable departure.

Rome clears the gap between us in two long strides. He cups my face and kisses me so hard; I am fairly certain my legs might go out beneath me. The feel of his tongue as it sweeps across mine with no hint of foreplay or apology reminds me that just because Rome is very much controlled in public, it does not mean he doesn't have a passion that scorches beneath the surface.

It's an unquenchable craze, the way we burn for each other.

14

MY MONSTER

COLETTE

Rome's fingers grip my body as if he is trying to hold himself back from devouring me whole. If vampires are thought of as monsters, then Rome is *my* monster, and I am his.

Though his kiss takes me off guard, my infatuation with him catches up easily. My fingers twine in his hair, not in the doting way I usually stroke him, but this time with a passion that's akin to anger. I wanted to be able to say those things to him directly, not to my brother, and then have Rome accidentally overhear. I want to live with Rome, to make his family my own, but the sheer impossibilities of that are too many to ever surmount.

If all we have are secret trysts and private kisses, then I will not waste this one. I will cherish each one because they are mine. We belong to each other, no matter that the world demands we sit at separate tables.

Rome's hand trills up my thigh under my skirt, thumbing the flesh because he knows there is no part of me I would not turn over right now. "I love you," he admits, stirring my stammering heart into a frenzy. "I love you and I would move in here if it was up to me. You know I want more than a drawer. I want a life with you."

Pressure builds behind my eyelids. Emotion threatens to kill the mood that's swept us completely from our melancholy. "Don't say it," I warn him as I nip at his lower lip. "Don't make me want this more than I already do. I'm mad for you, Rome."

He kisses me and fists his fingers in my hair, yanking my head back so my face is angled to his. "I fitted you with a tracker when I gave you that necklace, so I think it's safe to say I lost my grip on sanity weeks ago. I'm crazy for you, Coletta. Let me... Please, tré-sur. Let me talk to your family. I don't want to pretend with them."

My eyes squinch shut to fend off the bad idea. "No. I won't make you a target any more than you already are. You and my father are finally getting along and making real progress. We can't jeopardize that."

Rome steps forward with his hands still around me. His face burrows in the crook of my neck, kissing and sucking as only the best vampires know how to do. He backs me up until my legs hit the edge of my bed.

And suddenly, I'm falling.

I knew that if I ever did truly fall for someone, it would

have to be a crush that crashed my will to die alone. That was the plan all along.

But as Rome's lips make sweet love to my throat while I mewl atop the mattress, I know all my protests that would have me cling to sanity and decorum are dead on arrival. They are the last vestiges of a barrier that soon will come crumbling down.

"I love you," I tell him at the exact same moment he utters a breathy "I love you."

I feel something shift in the air, as if our simultaneous declaration of love has cracked open a mystical force that the universe reserves only for lunatics who love as recklessly as us.

My back arches for him. My lashes flutter because, of all the things Rome knows about me, my vulnerable spots are up at the top of the list. I am only helpless for him. I waste no time or energy regretting my surrender. I have no desire to be anywhere but with this incredible man. It's an addiction, I am learning, but each hit of him only increases my need for more of whatever this is.

Rome takes my bare leg and hooks it around his hips. My fluttery navy skirt slips up my thigh as if scandal is a thing we do not fear in the least. His weight atop my body is the comfort I need to keep me warm at night, so I tighten my leg around him, eliminating any gap between us. He is firm against the heated parts of me, driving me all the more wild when his hips press to mine. Each breath we take is done together, even though I am gasping through my desire.

My fingers make quick work of unbuttoning his shirt and tearing it down his arms. "I need you," I whisper.

Did we close the door?

Do we have enough time indulge in all that I crave?

All other questions fly out of my mind to make room for the lust that is taking me over.

His fingers are magic, slipping between us where they easily find their mark. Rome is a man who has never had to question his prowess.

My hips jerk against his while we kiss and caress, grab and gasp. "More," I beg.

Rome does not deny me when I reach for his belt buckle. My fingers are clumsy yet certain that this is what I want, and only with him.

He tears my shirt over my head because even the slightest scrap of fabric is too much a barrier between us. He pauses only the briefest of moments to admire me with a reverent expression before his features are taken over by an animalistic lust.

We see no need to be gentle with each other.

Heat coils in my belly as he lowers himself onto me, drawing energy in like a spring ready to burst through my ribcage.

Then suddenly, something booms. I hear the sound

and feel it in my brain. Like fireworks being blasted inside my ear canal, the sound makes me jump.

"What was that?" I ask him, barely pausing our kiss for him to work in a response.

"No idea."

This has happened before when our trysts grew heated. Each time, we pulled away, unsure what the foreign sound meant.

But this morning, neither of us has the self-control to pull away. I tighten my legs around Rome's waist, letting him play with the edges of my lacy underwear while I slide his trousers down his muscular thighs.

His tongue plunders my mouth as his hips move against mine. His breath is coming in heavier now, while my chest moves unevenly to keep up with our erratic rhythm of more, always more.

Suddenly Rome's gasps turn harried, his chest heaving like a runner on a cold day. "Coletta," he rasps, though the sound of my name on his lips is more a plea for help than an indication of pleasure. "No! Stop! No, we can't! It's not happening! It's not possible!"

The romance twists into something grim and terrifying when I can't hold air in my lungs. My breath syncopates without my permission, not like it should, but like it shouldn't unless there is a shortage of oxygen in the room.

Suddenly my grip on Rome turns to a panicked

pawing. My lungs won't expand enough to let in more than a fraction of the breath I need.

Terror courses through my bones. "Rome!" I cry out, though even that sound is choked. "Can't... breathe!"

Rome jerks his head up, breathless and confused as he clutches at his own chest. But the clear picture of his face blurs before my eyes, like someone brushed their hands over an oil painting that wasn't quite dry. His movements, though blurred, mirror mine—short of breath to the point of panic.

Rome rolls off me clumsily, his spine hitting the mattress while we both stare up at the ceiling, writhing as we gasp for breath, which slowly begins to come back to us.

I can barely put purpose to the many questions that tumble through my mind while my chest jumps. I'm fighting for clarity, for reason, but it comes slowly. Nearly a minute passes before my breathing settles back into a bearable rhythm.

Rome threads his fingers through mine. "Are you alright?"

"What was that?"

He doesn't answer, which does nothing to assure me. He merely runs his thumb over mine.

"Rome, what happened? There was a booming sound. I couldn't breathe, then I couldn't see straight."

"That's not what happened. Nothing happened. It was

a few kisses, is all. You're overreacting." My boyfriend drops my hand so abruptly that it almost feels like I am repellant to him.

I'm projecting. That can't be true.

"Rome, I..."

"You're imagining things."

"Imagining suffocating? Do you understand what my seizures can do if they go too far? I can stop breathing! But I didn't have a seizure, I don't think. Is that what's happening?" I examine my hands and then touch my face. "My meds. I need another pill."

"You're not... It's fine, but we can't do this ever again. I take it back. You're imagining..." He motions to the bed, as if to imply I invented our entire relationship out of my daydreams. "I got carried away. It won't happen again. This was a mistake."

I sit up halfway, leaning back on my elbows. "What?"

Rome's eyes are wide with fright. "All of it. I don't need a drawer. I can't stay here."

Rome rebuttons his shirt and pulls up his pants, turning his back on me. He trips over his own two feet as he parts from my side.

Serves him right.

He fists the door's handle. "I have somewhere I need to be. I just remembered. You'll need to meet with the mayor and the governor without me. Orlando can take you."

My mouth falls open as shock hits my system.

Did I miss a step?

Did I say something mean by mistake?

"Rome, wait!"

"I'll be out of town for a while." His words crash over my head like a ton of concrete.

I reach down and snatch up my shirt from the floor, tugging it over my head. "Are you serious? We have a meeting to go to right now."

"You can handle it without me. Or cancel and I'll deal with it when I get back. I have to go. We can't... I need space. That shouldn't have happened. I let things go too far."

"Wait! Rome, I..."

"No!"

It is the first time Rome has ever raised his voice at me.

The first and the last. I can see the fear in his eyes that mirrors my own. I am a wreck in the wake of his abruptly cold demeanor.

Before I can say another word, Rome turns his back on me. He doesn't leave, but stands in the doorway, taking his time catching his breath.

His body doesn't look strong right now, but like he is trying to force it to muscle through whatever we just endured together.

What is happening? My limbs aren't quaking, like they would if I was low on my meds; it's more that everything feels weighted and clumsy. It's like I am moving through gelatin.

Drunk. I don't drink often because alcohol mixes poorly with my medication, but I can imagine this is what it would feel like to have had three too many cocktails.

My voice embarrasses me almost as much as the plea that escapes my lips. "Rome, please. I don't understand."

But he doesn't give me the chance to make sense of any of this. His torso is tense, I can tell from his stilted gait. "You need to leave. Orlando doesn't like to be late."

And just like that, Rome exits my bedroom without looking over his shoulder.

As if I mean nothing.

As if *we* mean nothing.

Emotions, the likes of which I never dreamed I would aim at Rome, fill my soul. I am angry that he would dismiss me so thoroughly when it's clear something physiologically odd just took place. I told him I couldn't breathe, yet he is acting like I called him a hateful slur. I'm confused, unable to conjure up a reason why he might behave this way.

But beneath the anger and confusion is a hurt that horrifies me. I counted on us. I assumed we would be together through thick and thin. But there is no way I would tolerate linking myself to someone who gets up and leaves when I tell him I am having trouble breathing.

When I tell him I love him.

When I tell him I wish we could be married.

My skin feels cool now, the heat from our bodies dissipating into nothing, as if it never existed. I didn't realize just how fragile our connection was, that it could be brushed away in a breath.

Reality bears down on my shoulders, threatening to flatten all that I hold dear.

The front door shuts, letting me know Rome has left my home, and possibly my life.

15

FIGHTING FOR CHANGE
COLETTE

My entire being is numb, save for my feet that somehow understand they must move me forward. My hand is tucked into the crook of Orlando's elbow—not because I put it there, but because Orlando hasn't let an inch of space come between us since I emerged from my bedroom.

Lucky for me, Orlando is not a talker. After I told him he could leave and didn't need to come to the meeting, he responded by staring me down until I rolled my eyes at him, consenting to let him come along. He drove me to the meeting in silence, which was probably best. My limbs are functional, but still a little tipsy. I don't understand what happened to make my body like this, and I'm sure as heck not going to ask Orlando about it.

Orlando knows Rome ditched me for more than just

this meeting. I don't even want to make eye contact with Orlando, for fear of seeing pity in his eyes aimed my way.

We walk through city hall in silence toward the conference room. People whisper when they see me pass, but that's nothing new. They always gawk when they see the Last Deadblood. Or when they see a human near a vampire. But when they remember who my family is and who Orlando's family is, they go back to their whispering in lieu of the scandalized mute stares.

I'm not sure which one I prefer.

A nap. That's what I prefer. I want to lie down and not talk to anyone for a solid year.

Rome left me.

Today is the first time since I moved back to Mayfield that I have voluntarily traded my heels for flats. Orlando's form practically swallows mine as we walk in step, being that I am a scant five feet tall. After the kiss and the crash, and then Rome's prompt exit, I'm not as steady on my feet as I would need to be to rock stilettos.

Rome is gone, and I can't do a thing about it. I can simply put one foot in front of the other. Though right now, even that feels like a grand effort.

I am fighting for his people, and he can't be bothered to show up for our appointment?

Guilt taps me on the shoulder, reminding me that vampires are not "his people." They are *my* people, because they live in Mayfield, just like me. I am fighting for my neighbors (though, I'm sure they all wish I was dead, so they didn't have to worry about my toxic blood).

The receptionist greets us with manic head bobbing and wide eyes, directing us down the hallway.

I've said nothing yet, which I prefer. I figure the longer I can keep my mouth shut, the less apt I am to display my broken heart.

Not broken. Stony.

This is a dream. A nightmare. It must be. That Rome would walk out like that in the middle of...

The pain is too great to parse through, so I put one foot in front of the other, going where I am directed.

We are on time for the meeting, but it looks like we are the last to arrive—a fact that I know bothers Orlando, though he doesn't say anything about it. The room is filled with the mayor, the governor, three journalists, the city's treasurer, the head of the school board for the East End and the head of the school board for the West End, plus a number of secretaries.

There was not supposed to be this many people here.

Governor Ingrid Mason is an authority figure I have always admired. To be a woman in power who possesses infinite poise and grace while still maintaining her hold on the issues is a feat not many can achieve.

She took my phone call. She didn't scoff when I told her of my ideals.

She showed up.

I draw courage from the fact that she will not get in my way, and perhaps might even be on my side.

She would not let a flake of a man ruin her chances at establishing peace and moving the world forward. She didn't balk at my suggestions for Mayfield because I believe deep down in her heart, she wants this sort of thing to be put into motion.

She just needed someone to light the bomb who can get out of this mess without the thing exploding in her face.

Here we go.

There are two seats left at the head of the long oval table, meant for Rome and me. My heart hammers at conducting this meeting without backup. I worry the sound of my nerves has become audible, even as everyone at the table finishes introducing themselves. It's not until Orlando helps me to sit down that I realize I might have to explain Rome's absence.

"I will be speaking for the Valentino family today," Orlando informs the room. Instead of assuming his gargoyle-like position at the doorway, Orlando slides into the seat beside mine. He leans back in his chair, though not sloppily, and does his best to intimidate the room into silence while seated.

This, apparently, is a skill that translates well to any room, no matter if Orlando is sitting or standing.

The room goes quiet, and all eyes turn to me.

This is no time to clam up, so I strike forward, flipping open the portfolio that contains the copies of our plan. I pass them around while I pull out my notes, hopping on the first talking point without easing us in.

Let's get this over with.

Though I am not rude, I make it clear in my tone that I will be controlling the room today. We go point by point through my list, with the others asking only clarifying questions.

They turned into a cooperative lot after Orlando rested his arm across the back of my seat. It's a clear message to the room: utmost respect shall be paid, or Orlando will be displeased.

When Orlando is displeased, bodies disappear.

I have the beginnings of a headache, which mutes any attempts I might have made to be pleasant.

The head of the East End's school board scoffs at me. "But to ask the East End to give up a heavy portion of their funding? You can't be serious."

The man from the West End representing the school board is a fellow in his fifties called Christopher. He hasn't spoken yet, no doubt assuming my plan is sweet, but he holds no hope of it making it past this room. He doesn't speak in his school's defense. I'm guessing he lost the will to fight for justice a decade or more ago—back when the vampire children may have had a chance at a decent education. His complacent checked-out expression tells me he can't be the only one fighting for his kids anymore.

It's my turn now.

I take up the baton he shrugs at and prepare myself to beat the ignorance in the room to death with it.

...or perhaps I should do something less violent but equally effective.

I run my tongue over my top row of teeth, all diplomacy leaving me the moment Rome left Mayfield. "I don't much care where the funding comes from. If you need to slash the budget of the schools in the East End, so be it. If you need to allocate funds from somewhere else in the budget, fine by me. It's no concern of mine how you correct the problem. I am merely bringing it to your attention that this foolishness is over."

Perhaps I shouldn't be insulting the people whom I am hoping will be cooperative, but I have little in the way of sweetness lingering in what remains of my soul.

Marjorie, the head of the East End school board, sits up straighter. Her dyed blonde hair flips over her shoulder. "Then whom do you suggest I fire at my school to tighten our budget? Which teacher do you think is expendable?"

I scoff at her jab, seeing exactly how this bitterness will be replayed in the press if I don't get ahead of it all now. "I think you could learn a thing or two from Christopher on budgeting. I suggest that if you cannot figure out how to tighten your budget, you two merely switch funding. You'll make do with what he uses, and he will buy all sorts of non-essentials like books and whatnot with the budget you currently have."

The mayor and the governor are silent, watching the match like a game of tennis—the argument volleying back and forth.

Marjorie splutters her indignation. "That is the most ridiculous thing I've ever..."

"Then back to my original proposal that the budgets be split evenly between the two territories."

Marjorie collects herself, smoothing out the ruffles on the front of her blouse. "You don't know what you're talking about. We have a higher rate of graduation than they do in the West End. Our students have better test scores."

I lean forward and stage whisper to her, as if she is dense and can't see the proper answer, even when it is obvious. "You also have more books and teachers. I wonder if there's a correlation." I straighten my spine, maintaining an attitude about me that demands not just respect, but reverence. "You have more children in school because their families have enough money not to pull their kids out so they can get jobs and help support the household. Your schools have a higher rate of graduation because they have infinitely more resources to help those children. Your test scores are higher, forgive me, because you don't have thirty-five children crammed into each classroom. Your teachers are not pushed past their breaking point." I sit back, grateful for Orlando's arm around my chair. "Do you assume you can spout the talking points used to make the wealthy feel good about themselves to scare us into silence?"

"Us? You're human, Miss Kennedy! You're fighting for the wrong side." She scoffs at me and then looks around the room for validation.

I point at her, my voice deadly and quiet. "Right there is the reason why I am here. That attitude. The part of you that says we deserve more simply because we happen to have an advantage at this moment in time. The side I am fighting for is *all* students. All children. The fact that you think it is acceptable to only fight for children who look like you is appalling, and has been noted by everyone in this room."

Not like they're not all guilty of the same thing. Not like my unconscious bias hasn't tugged me in the same poor direction when I'm not careful to keep myself in check.

"Her name is not Miss Kennedy, Marjorie," Orlando corrects without holding back. "She is Madam Deadblood. You will not show her disrespect in my presence."

It's the only thing he has said in a while, yet it is the perfect chiding.

My mother was Madam Deadblood or the Last Deadblood when I was still referred to by the press as the Youngblood.

This is my time to take hold of the mantle and squeeze the corruption from this divided city.

Marjorie throws her arms into the air. "What are your qualifications? Why on earth are we sitting here, listening to her?"

I don't have it in me to smile, even if it's a wicked smirk. "Because the mayor and the governor are smart enough to understand that if you don't listen to me, the rest of the world will. No one cares about the vampires now, but if they get a good look at the abuse going on so near to their beloved Deadblood?" I shake my head and cluck my tongue at her. "I shudder to think the scrutiny your financials will be under then. I am giving you a chance to do the right thing. If you don't take this last warning and change things now, I am fully prepared to take this thing as far up the flagpole as it can go." I pause to examine my nails. "I wonder if you'll still have a job by the time I'm finished? If businesses are allowed to discriminate against vampires and not allow them entry, imagine what your salon, your grocer, your post office, your world will do to you once your corruption is exposed."

Marjorie gasps, scandalized that I have threatened her livelihood.

I have no qualms about any of it. My heart has dwindled down to nearly nothing, beating only for people who will never know it is me who fought for them.

Good. I don't want a single person to smile at me ever again.

I stand, and Orlando follows suit. I pick up my portfolio and make my way to the door. "I need to make a phone call. My time is valuable, so I trust you can get somewhere both fair and amicable by the time I get back."

The Mayor Stapleton finally speaks up. "And if we can't?"

I narrow my eyes in on him, enjoying his squirm. "If you cannot see that all taxpaying citizens of Mayfield are cared for, then perhaps you have finished serving your purpose in this office." I cast my judgment upon the room. "Your time might be over, but I assure you, mine is just beginning."

Orlando follows me as I stalk into the hallway, shutting the door behind us as the room erupts in a heated debate.

Even if we win this today, it is a small victory. It is one step forward in a backwards society.

Though I know I nailed the presentation, I feel nothing still.

Rome is gone, and part of me is lost, too.

16

DENIAL AND ANGER
COLETTE

I call Declan to cancel our dinner tonight, but he doesn't pick up, so I guess we're still doing that.

I cringe as Orlando pulls into my driveway. Every sound is too loud as my headache only seems to grow.

I know tonight is important to my brother, so it needs to be important to me. I don't have the wherewithal to cook. I'm not hungry in the slightest. In fact, other than the call to my doctor, I don't have the desire to speak to anybody.

"You did a good thing today," Orlando reminds me as he cuts the engine.

"Mm-hm. You, too. Next stop, sitting down with just the governor and the mayor to make sure appropriate funds are being allocated to the West End. We'll give them time to get themselves together. I'll knock them back down if they don't play ball." I pick up my portfolio, which feels heavier, even though we passed out all the printouts we came with. The weight of it now is from the city's budget, which will be my homework for the next week.

Orlando runs his hand through his thick, black hair. "I still can't believe you got the governor to come to the meeting. Who knew our governor cared about vampires? You'd never guess it from the lip service she pays us with zero action behind it."

I fight back a snort. "Governor Mason doesn't care about anything but the fun of the drama, so that's what we'll give her. If she truly cared, she would have leaned on Mayor Stapleton long before I moved back home. She'll sit back and clap while the mayor sweats. I don't need her to agree to anything; I just need her present, so the mayor can't blow us off."

"Effective." Orlando gets out of the car and opens the door for me, offering his hand to help me out of the backseat. He frowns at my fingers when he runs his thumb over them, as if uncovering a clue that troubles him. "You're cold."

I don't reply, but instead make my way to the door that leads to my house, surprised when Orlando follows behind. "Did you leave something inside?"

Orlando's expression is somber. "I'm staying with you until Rome comes back."

I flinch at my boyfriend's name. Though, given how

quickly he ran away, I guess that's not an accurate title for Mister Valentino anymore. "That's not necessary. Declan's on the schedule for tonight so he'll keep watch."

Orlando is not dissuaded, and steps into the house behind me without hesitation. "I'm going to take a look around the yard to make sure everything is okay before I settle in for the night."

"Orlando, seriously. You can't be here tonight. Declan is coming over and bringing a friend. It's sort of a family thing happening tonight, so you have to go home." I don't like being firm or dismissive with the man who has been nothing but helpful this entire time, but my tact has long since left the building.

Orlando narrows his eyes at me. "If you need a few hours with your brother, that's fine. I have work to do in the city anyway. But I'll be back by ten, and I'll sleep on the couch. Declan can have the spare bedroom."

I pinch the bridge of my nose. "Orlando, you're not on the schedule for tonight, and you know it."

Orlando's upper lip curls. "Do you think I care about a schedule? Rome told me to look after you, so that's what I'm doing."

My temper flares. "Then you can go. He left us high and dry today with no explanation. We were…" I nearly let myself delve into a rant, but then I stop myself short.

Orlando's brow raises. "What were you doing before he split?"

"Nothing."

I grimace at the obvious fib.

Orlando doesn't appreciate being lied to, especially not so stupidly. "He stumbled out of your bedroom looking like he'd seen a ghost. He grabbed his keys and all but ran out the door, telling me to watch you while he was gone. What happened?"

"Foolishness. Nothing worth remembering. I've forgotten him already."

Though, as I say those words, it's like I'm stabbing myself in the chest.

I lift my chin. "I think we might've broken up." I hate the slight tremble in my tone. I don't want to feel it, let alone make my insecurity obvious to someone as stalwart and professional as Orlando. "So you don't need to stick around out of some sense of misplaced loyalty. I am no longer Mister Valentino's concern."

Orlando's brows are pushed together even as he takes off his suit jacket and hangs it on the hook by the front entrance. "You must have heard him wrong. He wouldn't end things with you. He's smitten."

"I really don't have the patience to argue with you about this. I have a headache and my brother is probably on his way here now. I will have to pretend I'm all cheery when he gets here, so I prefer not to have had an emotional breakdown just before opening the door to let him in. Declan is a good brother; he can smell crippling depression on me a mile away."

Orlando stands in the entryway to my home, perplexed and silent while I bustle around the house, straightening up the few bits of clutter that managed to accumulate over the past couple days. I can't calm myself down, but I refuse to dig deeper into the hole of hollow memories that used to mean something to me. Right now is all about purging.

Orlando still has not moved from the entryway. He is motionless as he watches me with clear consternation on his face. He's not much of a talker, for which I am grateful.

I order takeout for Declan and his boyfriend, my stomach souring at the thought of eating a thing. Then I grab a box from the recycling and make my way through the bedrooms, picking up odds and ends that either belong to Rome or remind me of him. I've never done the breakup thing before, but this seems right. I don't want his stuff lying around here. I have things to do, which are harder with all this nonsense weighing me down.

The pillow Rome laid on last night has to go. His overnight bag is easy to get rid of; Orlando can take it tonight. A few notes scribbled on a pad of paper go into the box of crap. I refuse to waste time wallowing. This will be quick and boring. No one knew about our relationship; no one will know about our breakup. Easy-peasy.

I rush past Orlando, who still has not moved. When I drop Rome's overnight bag at his feet, Orlando tilts his head at me. "He's coming back, Coco."

"No, he's not, and even if he did, I wouldn't let him in the front door." And just like that, my heartbreak masks itself as anger. Rage is far more comfortable to touch than sadness. Anger snaps and dissipates over and over, giving you a break in between. Sadness can go on forever.

I don't have the time for that, nor does Rome deserve my sadness after leaving so abruptly.

Orlando runs his hand from his forehead to his chin. "Whatever happened between you two has gotten totally out of hand. I'll call him."

"Then I will be out of earshot. I mean it, Orlando. I don't want to hear his voice or his name. I've had a long day, and it's not over yet."

I storm to the second bedroom and slam the door because that is exactly how mature I feel like being right now. I don't want to deal with the world or with anyone, so I bury myself in numbers. The budget from the meeting today spills out over my desk, giving me something dense with which I can distract myself.

The columns make little sense to me because most of it is shorthand. I don't know what many of the columns mean, nor can I tell if each is worth the giant sum allocated for it.

I take a deep breath and start with the basics, going over the few things I can make out. I search the internet for the rest, making annotations as I go. My handwriting is tiny in the margins as I delve deeper into the mess of numbers. For the first time since this afternoon, I feel myself breathing. In and out, though there's still that tight band around my chest and pressure in my skull.

I will not bury myself in depression; I will bury myself in numbers.

My anger has a decent place to set up camp here. The budget for the city is completely skewed, earmarking far more funds per capita to the East End than the West. It's no real surprise, but to have the numbers laid out this clearly helps me focus my rage on something productive.

There is one thing that has me scratching my head, though. The beautification budget for the West End is zero. Not a single dollar from the city goes into making the West End beautiful. But I've seen commercial landscape done well over there. There are pockets of greenery littered throughout vampire territory, though it still is nothing as lush as the East End.

When my doorbell rings, I glance at the time on my laptop. An hour? I've been at this an hour? It feels like ten minutes. My headache is nowhere near dissipating, but on the bright side, I can pass off my lack of pep onto that instead of coming clean about the breakup in front of Declan and his new boyfriend.

When the front door opens, worry hits my system. I race to the entrance too late. "Sorry! Orlando was just leaving." I don't introduce Orlando to Declan's boyfriend because it's not my place. Nor is it my place to sweep their relationship under the rug.

Orlando frowns at me while Declan gives me a panicked series of blinks, paling at the unexpected fourth. "I'll be back at ten," Orlando announces. It's more of a warning than anything else.

"No need," Declan tells him. "I'm on the schedule for tonight. But thanks, man." He slaps Orlando's hand three times, reminding us all that they are old friends.

Orlando holds my defiant gaze. "I'm afraid the family insists I'm here. You can stay, Declan, but I'll be here, too." He reaches for his suit jacket. "I have a few things to take care of." He taps his wrist to remind me of the time. "Ten o'clock, Coco."

Orlando turns on his heel and exits without another word, leaving before he can experience the brunt of my rebuttal.

Declan escorts his boyfriend inside, shutting the door behind him. His eyes are wide but he doesn't voice all of his concerns. Instead, he frames them with bemusement. "Didn't realize Orlando would still be here."

"Sorry about that." I turn toward the breathless newcomer, commanding myself to give him my full attention. "You must be Lucas."

The man standing beside my brother is three inches taller than Declan, with skin a beautifully rich dark brown.

"It's nice to meet a family member. You'll have to forgive me if I say something stupid. I'm a bit nervous."

I was determined to like Lucas before I met him, but after his exposed nerves hit the air, I am glad to find that I don't have to put forth an ounce of effort. He is positively precious.

Lucas presses his thick lips together and then releases them over and over, letting me know that whatever has happened in my day previous to this, I need to put it aside.

My brother has a boyfriend now, which is cause for celebration.

17

MY BROTHER'S BOYFRIEND
COLETTE

I take in Lucas' admission of nerves, sizing up his tensed shoulders and overly bright smile. "I was just about to make some tea because I'm a little on edge myself. Is chamomile okay?"

Lucas nods with a pleasant air about him. "Absolutely. Thank you."

I take his coat and hang it up next to Declan's and mine, noting how nice it is to have my brother's boyfriend in my home.

Declan shoots us both a narrowed eye, his chin angled to the side in a slight scold. "Lucas hates tea. He's just being polite. You can be real around my sister. She doesn't care if you're more of a coffee person."

Lucas' neck shrinks as he shoves his hands into the pockets of his jeans. "Maybe it's just that I haven't found the right sort of tea yet. I'm happy to try something new."

I link one arm through Declan's and the other through Lucas'. "Let him be overly polite to me, Declan. Soon enough we'll get used to each other, and then I'll never get my way again."

Declan snickers as we walk to the kitchen together. "Fine, fine. Do you have a sweater or something, though? You're freezing. Did you just come in from a walk before we got here?"

My nose crinkles. "No. Am I really that cold?" I touch my fingers to my face, feeling a definite chill I did not notice before. "Then tea is the perfect thing." My mouth draws to the side as I migrate to the cupboard above the stove. "I'm not sure I have any coffee that's decaf."

Lucas reaches over my head and grabs down the chamomile. "I wouldn't drink it if you did. Now I'm willing to go to the mat on this issue. I *need* some chamomile tea. It might be the one thing my life has been missing."

I chuckle at his humor as I put water in the kettle. I ignore Declan's head shake because Lucas and I are bonding. It's new and it's fragile, but so help me, I will not let this day end until the two of us are best friends.

"Takeout is on its way. My plan was to put it in fancy serving dishes, so you thought I cooked it myself."

"I'll close my eyes and do my best pretending while you do exactly that." Lucas moves to the cupboard I point him toward and grabs down three mugs.

"No mugs tonight. You're what we call a fancy guest, so

we use the good China." I motion to the top shelf that I can't reach without a step stool.

Lucas studies the cup appraisingly. "I've never had tea in a legit teacup before. Maybe that's the one thing that's kept me from enjoying the wide world of tea."

"I'm positive it is. That's our mother's wedding China. Can you believe Declan and Fintan didn't want it?"

Declan plops down on the stool on the other side of the counter, his elbow resting on the flat surface. "I'm a neanderthal. It's what makes me so loveable."

I want to give a sarcastic laugh, but Lucas steals my breath when he smirks at Declan in this cutesy pie way, as if to say to my brother, "Loveable is exactly what you are."

I start making mental plans of having Lucas come over to my house for holidays until they're ready to come out to the family. Anyone who looks at my brother with a cherished respect like that is welcome to stick around until death do us part.

The delivery person arrives just as the tea starts to come together. Lucas makes a show of closing his eyes while Declan and I scoop the fried rice, lo-mein and orange chicken into my mother's fine serving dishes. She would be appalled, I'm sure, to see her wedding China used for takeout.

Or maybe she would laugh and get in on the joke, too. Maybe at the next meal, there would be fast-food hamburgers on the plates with limp fries.

The thing is, I don't know much about my own mother. Sometimes my imagination of her takes on the form of a female version of my father—always right, stubborn and disapproving. Then other times, I pretend I inherited the sillier and more resilient parts of my personality from her.

Though we've never been a faith sort of family, Declan and I both pause while Lucas prays over the meal. "Dear Lord, thank you for this food and for the company. Please don't let me break anything or spill anything. Amen."

The prayer is unpretentious and sweet, just like him.

The smell of fried rice always makes my mouth water, but tonight it doesn't have the same effect. Sure enough, when I take my first bite, the food tastes all wrong. It's bland where it should have the smack of salt, and bitter where the peas and carrots should add a pop of sweetness.

"What's that face for?" Declan inquires while he shovels down bite after bite.

"Nothing. The food doesn't taste right. I've ordered from them before, but maybe their chef is having an off night." I shrug off the fact that the meal tastes bad and eat enough to keep my stomach from complaining too loudly.

Though I nursed a catastrophic heartbreak earlier this same day, I play the part of the consummate friend and rabid interviewer. I ask how they met (at a coffee shop), where Lucas grew up (an hour south of Mayfield), what he does for a living (roofing), and what he does for fun (chess, skiing and snowboarding). I have no frame of reference for any of his hobbies, so I delve into those, asking technical questions of all sorts so he knows I am very much invested in getting to know him.

Of course I want to bond with Declan's boyfriend. But I'm also playing defense. If I keep the spotlight on Lucas, I won't have to answer any personal questions myself. I don't want him to know me. I don't want anyone to know me right now. My life is a scrambled mess, and I don't like to present myself that way.

My plan works brilliantly all through dinner. But the tides start to shift when the meal ends. Declan packages the leftovers and puts them in my fridge, humming to himself, which he always does when he's happy.

I wash the dishes by hand while Lucas dries. I listen with rapt attention while Lucas fills me in on the best restaurants outside of Mayfield. "We'll have to take you to our favorite place."

"You have a favorite place that I don't know about? For shame. I'm free every Wednesday, so pick your favorite Wednesday and we'll go."

Lucas chuckles at me. "Are you sure? Not everyone can handle the heat in their curry."

I bump my hip to Lucas'. "You drained your tea for me. I can breathe fire for you."

"Wednesdays?" Declan asks, straightening after sliding the last of the leftovers into the fridge. "I thought you had a thing on Wednesdays."

I keep my eyes on the suds, scrubbing the debris off the platter. "Not anymore. Free as a bird."

"Did you move your Wednesday appointment to a different day?"

Stop prying, Declan. "Nope. Just cancelled it. The client I was meeting with decided he wasn't interested anymore."

Declan's voice turns sharp. "Are you serious? And you're just now telling me this? That's an important change, Coco. How dare he?"

The mood changes from light to cloudy.

Lucas dries slower, catching the shift in the air.

My headache is clustered around my temples. "The client cancelled this morning, so I didn't have much time to fill you in. It's fine. Everything's fine."

Declan rears back. "Cancelled? I don't know what that means."

Lucas blinks at me and then turns to Declan. "It means they broke up."

I groan, dropping my head. "So much for our clever code. Can't believe you cracked that one."

Lucas chuckles while he dries the platter. "You should have said something. We didn't have to come over if you just went through a breakup. What happened?"

I don't want to shut down the conversation, but I really, really don't want to talk about it.

I muscle through the discomfort so I can be as honest as I dare with my new third brother. "We were making out.

Things got a little intense and he freaked out. Practically ran out the door. Said he was leaving town for a bit, cancelled our plans and told me I was making too much out of our relationship." I hold up my chin, daring Declan to call me out on my broken heart. "So that's that. A handful of months down the drain. There are worse tragedies to mourn, I'm sure. One of which is that I didn't order anything for dessert. Would you like some cookies? I have a box in the pantry."

There we go. Confess to the crime then change the subject. Dazzle them with sugar.

Lucas sets down the serving bowl after drying it. "I could go for some cookies and sympathy. Who is this fellow? I hate him already."

"He doesn't have a name," I declare for obvious reasons, my nose in the air. "We'll call him Keith. I've never met a sexy Keith, so there we go. Keith has no power here, so he doesn't need to be the topic of any conversation ever in my house. Cookies. That's what we should be talking about. Cookies deserve our full attention. Keith does not."

Lucas' full lips pull to the side, fixing me with brown eyes that hold no agenda, other than kindness. I can see why Declan is so taken with him. "That bad, eh? Alright, we don't have to talk about Keith. But we might have to defuse Declan. He looks ready to boil over."

Declan's fists are clenched at his sides. "Where is he?"

"Out of town," I repeat. "It's no business of mine where

he's gone. Keith is no one to me, and no one to you anymore, either."

"Fine. You won't talk, but I know someone who will. Excuse me. I've got a phone call to make."

"Who are you calling?"

"Either his family or a hitman. I haven't decided yet. Maybe his family, then a hitman, depending on how the first conversation goes."

I roll my eyes, though I know our family's proclivity for violence is something to take seriously. "Declan, honestly. People break up all the time. It's nothing."

Declan raises his voice, spooking Lucas, whom I can tell is not accustomed to the gloves-off family side of Declan. "*You* are not nothing! He told you he loved you. You were together, and for no obvious reason he ran out like a little baby because it all got a little too real for him? I'm not about to sit back and let him experiment being in a relationship with my sister if he's going to pull that garbage. He's an old man who should know better. If he wants in this family, he needs to have figured out his infantile hang-ups prior to being with you."

My headache is only compounded by Declan's volume. "This isn't what I want, Declan! Don't involve yourself. Seriously. I'm handling it. I'm handling it so well that you didn't even know until just now. It's nothing. *He* is nothing."

Though, even as I say this, my heart screams like it's

just been torn out and stomped on by one of my spiky heels.

Rome is not nothing. But if I am going to continue living a normal life without crippling depression, that's exactly what I will have to convince myself.

Declan turns on his heel and grabs his jacket, stalking out of the house in a huff.

Embarrassment floods me at having my brother step in like that. I would call it overstepping, but truthfully, I would probably behave the same way if anyone ever treated Declan like that. "I, um... Sorry about that. I didn't mean to..."

Lucas moves over to the stove and refills the kettle, then turns on the burner. "I'm thinking this is the sort of evening tea was invented for."

I love that he's not making me talk more about this. I get out the milk and sugar. We stand in silence, letting the discomfort settle without brushing it away as most are wont to do.

Lucas fishes through my tea selections, reading the descriptions to himself. He keeps his eyes on the label when he finally speaks to me. "Declan is very protective of you."

I snort without a hint of happiness. "No kidding."

"He's afraid of your father, wary of Fintan, but he adores you."

My voice comes out quiet and with less attitude this time. "I love him, too. He's my best friend."

"Then you understand that he worries about you. It's not because he thinks you're weak or stupid. It's because if anything crushed you, he would be alone in the family again. When you lived overseas, those were his hardest years. At least, that's what he told me."

I swallow hard, my eyes focused on the kettle while it heats. "I feel the same way." I sigh, letting out a bit of the heaviness that's threatened to bury me where I stand. "I really didn't see it coming today. I've never been broken up with mid-makeout. I don't understand what happened. I'm not sure I want to."

Lucas selects a mint tea from the box. "I think we can let Declan deal with the headache of it all for now. We have tea to drink and cookies to eat." Lucas holds out one arm to me, inviting me in.

I don't hesitate to fold myself into his side. He's tall, like Fintan, but with a bit more bulk around the middle that makes him extra cuddly. His arm falls around me, squeezing with no intention other than to communicate sympathy and kindness. With his free hand, he picks up the pen hanging near the notepad on the fridge. "Here's my number. When you want to talk about it, I'll listen. I'll drink tea until I learn to like it, and we'll cry until all the tears that belong to Keith run dry. Deal?"

I squeeze his middle, wondering if all relationships end up leaving a girl feeling empty and soulless. "Deal."

Though I wish I could fix everything that's gone wrong, one thing is clear to me: Declan is in good hands with Lucas.

18

ORLANDO'S HOMEMADE REMEDY
COLETTE

Though Declan put up a good fight, Lucas was crucial in coaxing my brother to leave my house in Orlando's hands for the night. "I want a phone call if her ex-joker shows up. I want a phone call and for him to wait on the porch until I get here. I mean it, Orlando."

Orlando quirks an eyebrow at my brother, silently asking Declan if he truly believes a Valentino might take orders from him. "Goodnight."

It's as civil as Orlando can be, which I appreciate. I'm just as grateful when Lucas leads Declan down the front porch steps and into his car. He gives me an understanding nod, letting me know he will find a way to talk Declan down from his rage.

I really like Lucas.

Orlando and I don't speak much, communicating in

half-sentences and grunts only when absolutely necessary. I change into my warmest flannel pajamas while he surveils the perimeter before locking the house up for the night.

After an hour of tossing and turning in bed with sleep nowhere in sight, I get up and go to the living room, turning on the television for no reason other than to give myself an excuse to stay awake that isn't my headache or heartbreak. I keep the volume low, so I don't wake Orlando, who has taken up residence in the spare bedroom.

At this point, it has become Orlando's bedroom.

I'm not ready to miss Rome, because that would mean forfeiting my anger for a smidgen of sadness. Instead, I flip through the channels until I find something mindless to distract me from my grief.

My stomach growls, but nothing sounds appetizing. Even though I am dressed in long flannel pajamas, there is still a chill in my bones I cannot shake.

I manage to doze off on the couch at around three o'clock in the morning, awaking to a crick in my neck.

As much as I would like for that to have been my only rough night of less-than-spectacular sleep, the next three evenings are spent in much the same way.

On the fourth night, when I go out to watch television at midnight, Orlando is occupying my usual space on the couch.

"Oh, sorry. I didn't realize you were up still."

Orlando hands me the remote. "Your pick. I can't seem to land on anything entertaining."

I sit beside him on the couch, pulling my knees up like a cat on the cushion. "That's what you're doing wrong. Don't look for entertainment when you're having trouble sleeping. Fish for mindless. There are plenty of mindless distractions to choose from."

"Fair point."

We sit in silence for a few beats until I land on a crime scene show with a PG rating.

Orlando hands me the blanket on the arm of the couch, as if he knows that I have been perpetually freezing for days. "Your fingers are icy still."

I shrug. "It's winter. Or almost winter."

Orlando keeps his eyes on the screen. "You don't eat much anymore."

I frown that Orlando and I have spent so much time together that he's picking up on the details. "Maybe I'm coming down with a cold or something. Food tastes weird lately. I thought it was bad Chinese food at first, but even my normal meals taste off." I bury my body under the white fleece blanket. "It's no big deal. I'm not wasting away or anything."

We watch television in silence, though not uncomfortably so. Orlando's eyes shift to me every now and then, but he keeps quiet until I call him out.

"If you want to say something, say it."

"You're remarkably unaffected by Rome leaving. I'll admit, I was bracing myself for the waterworks."

I keep my tone laced with boredom, trying not to let the sound of my ex's name rattle my insides. "Yes, how glamorous it is to be able to compartmentalize. It's one of my most notable talents. My father sends me away for years and I pretend it doesn't bother me one bit. Fintan tries to auction me off to the highest bidder, and I laugh it off." I coil the blanket tighter around my curled-up form. "I learned a long time ago that crying doesn't do anybody a lick of good. Life will spit you out when it wants to, and there's nothing you can do about it."

Orlando studies my face. "That's pretty grim. I guess I always pictured you as the sunshine and rainbows type of girl."

I keep my eyes on the screen. "That's a nice picture. I suppose I should like to be the kind of person who believes in rainbows, but whenever I try, I usually get kicked in the teeth."

Orlando stands and stretches. "Do you have a heating pad around here somewhere?"

"Sure. In the bathroom cabinet. Is your back bothering you?"

"No more than usual." He moves down the hallway, looking kind of adorable in his white t-shirt and black pajama pants. It's not a huge departure from his daywear if I blur my vision slightly.

I wonder when the last time was that Orlando took some time off for fun. I can't even picture what that might look like.

He rummages in the bathroom and then the kitchen while I try to warm up under my blanket. The show I'm watching isn't interesting in the slightest. The puns are deadpanned and dreadfully dull, and the violence is off-screen. I want to get some sleep, but I'm tired of tossing and turning in bed.

I've taken to wearing flats at the salon. If that's not a sign that I'm tired and lost, I don't know what is.

When Orlando returns, he's got the heating pad over his shoulder and two teacups on saucers. Though I'm not particularly parched, I thank him for the thoughtfulness all the same. "You don't have to wait on me."

"I'm not. I was making myself some tea. It's just as easy to fix two cups. Lean forward."

"Huh?"

He sets the tea on the coffee table and puts a hand on my shoulder, tilting me forward. The heating pad is fresh from the microwave and slides blissfully down my spine. Orlando leans me back and resumes his spot next to me without a word.

I blink at him, trying to understand why he's being so helpful. "You don't have to..." But the heat hits my tailbone before my protest can fully come to light. "Oh, that's incredible. I didn't realize how cold I was." Pure warmth races up my spine, relaxing the tight hold I've had on my body for several days now. "You're a genius, Orlando."

He presses a teacup into my hands. "Drink up. Warm inside, warm outside. Then we're going to sleep. We're not waking up half a dozen times in the night to pace through the house. Actual sleep."

I take his scolding with zero rebuttal. I have been pacing at night during my fits of unrest.

The first sip of the chamomile introduces a flood of heat the likes of which I haven't felt in days, though it doesn't burn my tongue. From my face to my toes, there is nothing but a gooey warmth that infiltrates the chill in my bones.

Gratitude fills me as my muscles finally start to relax. "Whatever you did to this tea, don't tell me. Just make this for me every night, and I'll be your best friend forever. Extra honey?"

"Something like that." He watches me drink while he sips from his cup. "Glad it's working." Though, he doesn't look glad. If anything, it's as if he has been waiting for some sort of grim sign, which my love of this tea has somehow confirmed for him.

Whatever. I'm warm for the first time in days. My limbs begin to relax, and finally, my eyelids are heavy. "What did you put in this?" I ask him. I don't feel as if I've been drugged exactly. More like there is some sort of medicine in my tea that fixes what's felt so off.

"Homemade remedy."

I've seen Orlando in the middle of many stages of disaster before. Never once did he look scared. But as he stares at the television, sneaking glances at me every few seconds, there is true worry in his eyes.

Part of me wants to ask him about it, but the other part of me knows that if Orlando is scared about something, we are all doomed.

Still, I sip my tea, letting his homemade remedy seep through my bones and mend what I thought might never be repaired.

I don't care that... Keith... is gone. I am finally relaxed.

19

CRAZY COOKIES
COLETTE

Orlando and I fall into a rhythm over the next two weeks. Like an old married couple, we go about our separate lives during the day, and then have dinner and tea at night. He has taken both my brothers off the list of people to watch my house, making sure he is the only one in my space when the moon comes up.

We've become so in sync that I swear I knew he would have a tender tummy last night, so I made chicken noodle soup in a big pot. Then I made rosemary crackers from scratch. I don't know why I assumed this, but it turns out my guess was spot on.

Orlando has very few obvious emotions, but when he came home and saw the simple spread, I swear his eyes watered with appreciation.

We don't talk much about feelings or anything mushy —neither of us are in the mood for such conversations—

but there's an understanding we have achieved with very few words. I know when he's worried, when he's down, and when he's had a big accomplishment. He doesn't ever feel happy, I don't think. I'm not sure that word is in his vocabulary. He's not unhappy, but more mute about such self-gratifying things. There is pride and shame, but nothing as quaint as happiness.

I don't know why, but this stuck in my brain all day while I was at the salon.

Each time Orlando brings up Rome's name, I shut down the conversation. But that's the only almost-fight we've had so far. I have a feeling he would do the same if I asked him what makes him happy.

I noodle over the simple conundrum, picking the problem apart in my brain to see if I touch down on something that sparks with potential. While I know each person is responsible for finding their own happiness, there's something intriguing about introducing a friend to the concept which is so foreign to him.

Aside from the soul-crushing breakup, I feel physically better than I have in years. Even during the meeting with the powers that be when we discussed the city's budget, my hands don't tremble once.

Maybe I am getting better at stepping into my mother's shoes.

Or perhaps there is more to Orlando's homemade

remedy that he brews me every night than a simple dash of honey.

I don't want to think about that. I'm going to take the good luck as it comes without looking too closely at the details.

My plan is to beat Orlando home tonight, my fingers itching to get into the kitchen. It's odd, because I've been on my feet all day. Usually I would want nothing more than to sit down. I have a fair amount of paperwork to go over, too. The Secretary Treasurer of Mayfield wasn't exactly thrilled that I tore apart his budget.

Then again, if he didn't want me to dismantle his hard work, he should have done a better job doling out the city's funds.

The press is getting quite the education on budgetary matters. Every meeting produces more corruption, lined with a new way forward that I force people down in a cool and collected way they cannot protest without sounding crazy.

Declan calls me on my way home from the salon. "You doing okay?"

My mouth pulls to the side as I flick my turn signal. "Are we just foregoing the pleasantries now? No 'hello,' just straight to worry mode?"

"Sorry. Hello. Are you doing okay?"

"The third meeting with the Secretary Treasurer and his

staff went well. I am proud to report that I didn't throw anyone through the window, though the thought did occur to me. I have a feeling the next meeting is going to be our last."

"Throwing in the towel already?"

"Not exactly. I'm not in the business of wasting my time. Three meetings are more than enough to be able to land on something fair for the entire city. It's ridiculous that it wasn't done correctly in the first place. If we don't land on something this Friday when I go in next, I'll know they're jerking me around. Then the gloves come off."

"I can't believe how much you've already done so far. I knew you were mad at the system, but it's been a while since I saw you go on a tear like this."

I flip my hair over my shoulder. "I don't go on tears. It's all very controlled."

"Oh, that's my favorite part. You're the picture of poise while you rip them to shreds. Remember when they tried to force the janitor of the school into early retirement? You had that same sort of deadly calm to you."

"That's me. Calm and deadly."

Before I can ask Declan about his day, he pushes into my sore spot. "Have you heard from Rome?"

My teeth grit together. "No, and I wouldn't pick up the phone if he called. It's over. I hear from him as often as you do—as often as any Kennedy would. Please stop saying his name. You know I don't like it."

"He's supposed to have his biweekly meeting with Dad

tomorrow at your salon. Ro—your ex-joker—cancelled the last meeting with dad, but he didn't cancel anything this time." He lowers his voice. "Dad said Nico is taking the meeting instead. He's not too thrilled about the switch."

My neck shrinks. "I left a message with the sheriff, asking him to move the location. Hopefully he checks his voicemail."

"Odds of that are as good as a flip of a coin. You know how Dad is with phone calls that aren't from the precinct."

My only answer is a tired sigh.

Declan doesn't let me off the hook. "I'm a little worried about you. I don't think you're doing a breakup right. You're supposed to get all depressed and eat a quart of ice cream. Then we burn all of his things and go out drinking."

All of those things sound perfect, but I can't let my brother know that. "If my relationship meant nothing to him, then I don't see why I should carry on about it. There's nothing of his to burn; I boxed it all up the day he split and sent it home with Orlando." Declan is making me feel when I don't want to. As I turn onto the next street, I make the mistake of cradling my broken heart instead of shoving it into a box. "Before it came to a screeching halt, he asked me if he could keep his things in a drawer here. We said 'I love you.' Next thing I know, he's gone."

I can tell Declan is grateful I am opening up, even if it's only a few sentences. "What a child."

"Yes." I straighten, not wanting to open my heart an inch further, even if it's to clear out the mold that's starting to grow. "I don't feel like wallowing over foolishness. I have things to accomplish. A city to change. A business to run."

"It sounds like he committed too hard too fast and then spooked himself."

"Yes. Quite the mystery he is to himself. Fortunately, I don't have the patience to sit around and wait for him to grow up."

Declan pauses before he scolds me. "You're being a little harsh."

"I'm being what I need to be. Do you want to find me sobbing into a quart of ice cream? Do you want me to wallow and guess at the reason why he left when it is perfectly clear? He didn't love me. I am the same person in his eyes as I am in everyone else's: I'm a novelty."

Declan's tone sours at my phrasing. "You don't mean that. Rome wouldn't have stuck around this long if you were something sparkly and nothing else. He's too serious for that."

"Mister Valentino is a conqueror," I correct my brother as I pull into my driveway. "Once he got me, the fun was over. And I asked you not to say his name." I let out another labored sigh. "You're going to give me a complex. I don't care about any of it."

"Yes, you do."

"Well, I don't want to. Fake it till you feel it, right?"

"If you say so. Just say the word, and Lucas and I will be there. Is Orlando getting on your nerves yet?"

"Nah. He's a bit of a chatter box, but other than that, he's fine." It's an obvious joke, being that trying to get five sentences out of Orlando at a time is a feat of endurance. "I'm home now. Talk to you later."

I end the call, knowing exactly what I want to do.

The second I step foot into my house, I set the music blaring. It's nothing I care about listening to; it's just loud. I want noise and anger, which the metal station gives me in spades. It's only at night when things get quiet that I can't shut out the heartbreak.

I don't want to be weak. I spent too long being pitied and barely able to walk. A stupid breakup from a stupid boy isn't going to have the same effect on me that head trauma did. Not on my watch.

I'm not hungry. Or rather, I am hungry, but nothing sounds good. My taste buds are different now. It's been two weeks, and food still tastes weird. Not bad exactly, just off. Eating has become more of a checklist item than a thing of enjoyment or indulgence. The only thing that tastes right is the tea Orlando makes for me every night. Actually, it's better than good. It's an emotion all its own. The tea is sanity.

Sanity and honey.

I still don't want to know what he's putting in it that calms me so.

Instead of delving into the piles of paperwork I need to examine, I linger in the kitchen. I'm not sure why, but the urge to make oatmeal raisin cookies taps me on the shoulder. I haven't baked cookies in ages. In fact, I haven't baked sweets at all since I moved back to Mayfield.

I should shower and get off my feet, but before I can stop myself, I'm pulling down flour and brown sugar. Even though I am freezing and need to put on a sweater or something, I can't stop. It's as if my moves are predetermined, and my body is merely along for the ride. There's a need in me to make these cookies, though I still couldn't say why. I don't want to eat any. In fact, I have the strong urge to curl up in my bed and give in to the creeping depression I have been trying to push away.

It's hard pretending to the world that I don't care. That I don't need. That I don't want.

It's even harder to pretend to myself.

Yet even though I have no desire to be upright, I continue dumping ingredients into the bowl. Odder still, I don't use measuring cups or a recipe. It's like my hands know what they want to do. My brain doesn't need to be in charge anymore.

I feel like I am a marionette for someone else's mind. I'm sure I could stop, but I don't want to. I need to make these cookies.

I've never added caramel corn to an oatmeal raisin cookie. I don't even have caramel popcorn in the house.

That doesn't seem to be a problem. I have popcorn kernels, baking soda, butter, brown sugar, and vanilla.

Apparently, I now know how to make caramel popcorn.

Fear taps me on the shoulder. This isn't my recipe. I've never had oatmeal raisin cookies like this, and I don't really have a taste for them now. But I keep going, despite my growing anxiety that something dark is at work here. I could stop, but I want to know what is so important about these cookies. I need to know if this will turn out and become something good.

Perhaps I truly have cracked. One of my worst fears is that one day my brain will betray me again. Enduring a traumatic head injury does a number on a girl. Though I've passed all the cognitive tests out there, the worry that I will end up back in a wheelchair is a horror that's grown too big to compartmentalize.

I haven't cried in weeks. I refuse to give Mister Valentino even one tear. Yet as I toss the freshly made broken-up caramel popcorn into the batter, new tears fall into the bowl. My lower lip quivers as I start to sob over the ingredients.

20

FINALLY CRACKING

COLETTE

It's finally happened. I've cracked. There's something irreparably wrong with my brain.

And I am alone while my mind deserts all higher reason.

Despite my pride, I pull out my cell phone, my voice catching as I wait for my brother to answer. "Declan?" There's no point holding a stiff upper lip now. "Declan, can you come over?"

"Of course. Am I picking up ice cream?"

"No. I need... I think there's something wrong with my brain."

The second the horrible words hit the air, an agonized cry rips out of me.

"What? Coco, what happened? Did you fall? Are you taking your meds like you should?"

I nod, but then remember he can't see me. "Just come over. I'm scared."

I'm scared because I made cookies? I'm scared because apparently it was buried in my brain that I know how to make caramel popcorn? I'm scared because... because...

I end the call before my brother can bear witness to my complete mental breakdown. I want to run away from the batter, but there is a need to finish this project. These cookies are important, more so than anything I could be spending my focus on. The "why" doesn't seem to be an issue for the urgency of the moment.

The second the two sheets of cookies slide into the oven, I fall to my knees, holding my face in my hands so I can have a good cry.

These tears are not for Mister Valentino. They shouldn't be for him, at least. I should only be mourning the loss of my higher brain reasoning that has led me to this madness.

The nasty voice in my head chirps in my ear like the middle school bully who never left me alone. *"You're going to die alone,"* it tells me, kicking me when I am already sufficiently down for the count.

I catch my sob in my hand, unable to talk myself away from this ledge from which I have clearly already jumped. Sanity seemed so important, but now it's a distant memory. I am going to be the woman who does odd things she cannot explain because the voices in her head told her to.

This time it's baking cookies. What will my brain make me do next?

And I can't seem to stay warm. The tea Orlando gives me heats me back up, but by the next night, I start to get icy again.

I press my palms to the outside of the oven, willing the heat to ground me as much as it is able.

I cannot keep going like this. My body finally has turned stable and steady, but my mind has clearly cracked in some irreparable way.

I can't lose my mind now. Not when the officials of Mayfield are starting to listen to reason. There is too much to accomplish, too many wrongs to right.

When the cookies come out ten minutes later, the urge to throw them in the garbage tempts me. Instead, I move them to the cooling rack and drag myself into the shower. I wish my tears would stop, but even as I soap up, they fall down the drain with the remnants of my pride.

This is the problem with extreme compartmentalizing. The goal is to run away from sadness, so it doesn't have a chance to touch you. Apparently, I can run for a solid three weeks, but then I hit my breaking point. Even after I am clean, I sit in the tub under the hot spray, willing it to warm the parts of me that have iced over. I don't want to be cold to the brighter things in life. I don't want to be numb to opportunity and call it peace. I want...

I want...

I hate myself for wanting Mister Valentino. Even now, after he's left me and has made it clear he has no intention of coming back, I miss his face.

The way he smiled only for me.

The way he towered over me.

The way his presence made it seem like there was nothing at all in the universe that needed fixing if he was near.

I even miss his fangs. I never thought I would say that to myself, but it's true. The ridges I felt when his mouth was pressed to mine felt like we shared a secret that was dangerous to the world, yet sacred to us.

I sit in the shower until the water runs cold, reminding me that I cannot hide in here forever. Though, that notion holds a glittering appeal.

It's an effort to hoist myself up, dry off and get dressed. I miss my mother horribly, even though I'm sure that's not quite the sentiment weighting me most. I cling to the idea of having a mother, someone to shoulder the burden of heartbreak and hardship without fear of judgment. I picture her having an antique handkerchief with her initials embroidered on the corner with which she would blot my tears.

Maybe that's not how all mother-daughter relation-ships go, but in my imagination, ours would be exactly that.

I pull on my fuzziest pink pajama pants—the ones I

only wear when I can barely move. Though my limbs haven't locked up on me at all (in fact, they feel more flexible and strong than ever), my soul took a beating today. My silk camisole does its fair job of convincing me I'm a woman, but the conviction is muted when I push my arms into the sleeves of my bathrobe.

I don't want to wallow, but it seems a night of devastation is unavoidable.

Declan lets himself in, calling through the house for me. "Coco? I'm here, kiddo."

A deep inhale and exhale are necessary before I move down the hall into the living room. "You're going to regret coming over. I'm not very good company tonight."

Declan takes a pint of premium ice cream out of a grocery bag. "I'm really okay with that. What I'm not okay with is you going through this alone." He sets the ice cream down on the coffee table and motions me forward. My brother's arms fold around me while he rests his chin atop my head. "You're new to breakups, so you don't know the perks."

"I cannot imagine any possible perks right now."

"You're so lucky I'm here. Tonight, we're eating our weight in ice cream. We're going to burn all his things. We're going to talk about all the reasons we hate him and why he's not good enough for us. Then we'll get all sad remembering the good times."

I snort at his plan. "Then what?"

"Then we wait for the sun to rise. May not happen tomorrow, but one day, it will."

I burrow my face into my brother's shoulder. This was something I missed terribly while I was overseas. Declan and I are the only huggers in the family, so we cling to each other perhaps a little too tight. I don't want to need a hug to tether me to the planet, but without one right now, I fear I might float away on a sea of depression.

Declan seems to understand me enough not to let go. "Come on, kiddo. Let's find a comfy spot in the living room and unpack it all."

Declan leads me to the couch, careful with my body as he helps me sit down. He is used to my form being fragile, but tonight it's my insides that feel on the verge of shattering. He is careful with both, for which I am grateful.

Over the next half an hour, I fill my brother in on the bits of my relationship that he missed when I was still hiding it all in the beginning. The sweet touches, the first kiss, the many secret rendezvous at the beach—each moment once something to treasure. Now it's an embarrassment I cannot believe I tolerated.

"If this is what being in love feels like, I think I'm a one and done kind of girl. I am not putting myself through this again."

Declan brought the ice cream for me, but I'm not hungry for it, so he has polished off a third of the carton on his own. "Enjoy your lukewarm life, then. Did you feel anything so strong as when you were in love with him?"

I motion to my face and then bunch up my hair to wind it into a bun atop my head. "No, but a punch in the face is strong. That doesn't mean you should pursue it."

Declan snorts as he stands to put away the ice cream, which is now mostly mushy. "Next time, maybe you'll find a boyfriend who is a human. Might make things less complicated. Also, not to start in on bashing your ex so soon, but he has no idea how to be in a relationship. He's psychotic." Declan holds up his hands. "Not that I think that's always a bad thing. Part of that is par for the course, being that he has to clean up the mess his father left him. But just because he's good at his job doesn't mean he knows how to turn all that off and do a relationship right."

My nose scrunches. "I guess I never thought of that before. You're not wrong."

Declan's hand goes over his heart as he feigns a swoon. "I love to hear you admit that. Better than a birthday card."

When a key jangles in the front door, Declan immediately stands and puts his hand on his belt. I hate that he carries, but I get it. I don't like that he's on edge in my home.

Not that I can blame him. Wherever I'm at is usually the worst place for a person to be if they're looking for an uneventful haven.

Declan's shoulders lower. "Oh, it's just you. Hey, Orlando."

Orlando nods once to Declan. They slap each other's hand three times in greeting. "I'm still staying here tonight, Declan. I told you that I would be taking over the shifts from now on."

It's slightly less than a cheerful greeting, but that's my big sweetie pie for you.

Declan moves toward the kitchen. "I'm getting some water. You want any?"

I shake my head.

Orlando toes off his boots. "I'll make your tea in a minute. Let me warm up first."

"You don't have to do that, Orlando. You barely stepped in the door." Though we both know my words are just for show. All I want, all I'm thirsty for is the tea Orlando makes me.

Orlando doesn't reply, but continues on as he pleases, which is to move to the kitchen the second his shoes come off so he can set the kettle brewing.

Gotta love him.

Declan sits back down, his hand coming off the hilt of his gun. I wonder when my brother's life will be peaceful enough that he won't reach for his weapon when the door-knob rattles.

My angst softens the smallest bit. It's weird that Orlando's presence adds calm to the room. I'm sure I am one of the few people in the world who feel a sense of serenity in the formidable enforcer's presence.

"When was the last time you ate a meal?" Declan asks me. "You didn't touch the ice cream. You're thinner in the face than when I saw you last. Should I be worried?"

"I'm all grown up, Declan." I chuck his shoulder good naturedly. "I had lunch. I'll have dinner later. Had to put off my meal to accommodate my breakdown."

I ate the lunch Orlando packed me, but I don't mention that. I make Orlando and myself breakfast, and he makes us sandwiches for our lunches. He sends over a decaf cinnamon vanilla latte halfway through the day, and we take turns fixing dinner. Odd that we never discussed any of this; it just happened. It's this pleasant little rhythm that makes breathing a little easier.

"Colette!" Orlando's volume is rarely raised, so when he shouts his alarm from the kitchen, I'm on my feet and darting toward him. He sounds scared, like he's seen a ghost.

"What? Orlando, what's wrong?"

Declan's hand is on the hilt of his gun again, which amps up my nerves as I move through the house.

Orlando is staring at the cookies on the cooling rack as if I've baked a bucket of snakes and called it caviar. "Who did... Who gave you the... Why did... How..." He turns to me, his face ashen. He looks like a scared little boy, raw and anxious. "Did you make these?"

I swallow hard and nod slowly. That's all I am willing to admit to. Anything else will make me sound crazy.

Orlando looks at the cookies as if they are the key to his soul—a thing most people would debate he was born without. "My mother used to... Are these oatmeal raisin cookies with caramel corn in them?"

Declan's face pulls. "What? Why? That sounds way too sweet. Gross."

I gnaw on my lower lip. "I just felt like making cookies."

"But who told you to make these? Is this how your family makes oatmeal raisin cookies?"

Declan snorts. "Dad's never made cookies in his life. He's a meat and potatoes kind of guy."

"Then who? Did one of my cousins find a recipe for these and give them to you? Did my uncle teach you how to make them?" Then he frowns. "But he never made these. They were only my mom's."

I tug on my fingers, anxious because it feels like I did something wrong. "I didn't know they were your mother's recipe, Orlando. I never cooked with Aunt Gianna, and I don't remember her making these for me."

Declan frowns. "That's a weird coincidence."

"I'm sorry, Orlando. I hurt your feelings, I can tell. Made you think of your mother out of turn. I didn't know. I just had the urge to bake cookies, and this recipe popped into my head. I didn't even know how to make caramel corn, but apparently I'm a natural at it."

Declan plucks up a cookie and pops it into his mouth. "You made caramel corn? That's a step up from store-bought. Look at you, fancy chef." His eyes roll back as he lets out a noise of indulgence. "Mm. These are amazing."

"Oh, good. I was too afraid to try them."

Orlando turns his chin toward me. "You wanted to make cookies—my mother's recipe that you didn't know— but you didn't want to eat any?"

I shrug. "You know my taste buds have been off lately."

Orlando reaches out and lifts one off the rack, sniffing it with his eyes closed. The first bite makes his shoulders droop, his chin lowering in reverence. It's strange watching Orlando enjoy a cookie. It's akin to watching him ride a kid's tricycle, or perhaps it's like watching him attempt to pray.

He takes off his suit jacket and drapes it across one of the seats at the counter. He sits on the stool beside it, his eyes on the granite. "I wasn't sure what was happening, but that seals it. It can't be happening. There's no frame of reference for it, but there's no other explanation."

The tea kettle whistles, so I turn it off and cast around for the teacups he set out. I pour the hot water in, but the fragrance isn't the same. How is it Orlando pours hot water in a fashion superior to me? "Orlando, you're going to have to stop speaking in code."

My big sweetie pie shakes his head, looking positively haunted. "We shouldn't talk about this. But I don't see how we can get around it. It's impossible, but..."

"What?" Declan is on edge now. He steps closer to me, readying to shield me from mere words.

"You might want to sit down for this one," Orlando warns. "If you thought life couldn't get worse, I'm about to prove you wrong."

My stomach drops while I wait for Orlando to break my world all over again.

21

VAMPIRE BIRDS AND THE BEES
COLETTE

Orlando asked me to sit down, but I can't. I'm too stressed by his non-explanation. He knows how strange it is that I knew his mother's cookie recipe without having heard of it or tried it before. He has answers, yet he sits at the counter in my kitchen, muttering non-explanations that don't do me a lick of good.

"Spill it, Orlando," Declan demands, though not unkindly. "Why is my sister freaked out over cookies, and why do you look like you might cry after eating one?"

Orlando keeps his eyes from me. "How much do you know about vampires mating?"

Declan and I look at each other. It's not what either of us were expecting Orlando might say.

Declan's face pulls. "Uh, not much. It's not all that common, from what I remember. Occasionally a vampire couple mates. They have a more intense connection. Like they're the only two people on the planet or something. I dunno. Romance movie stuff."

"Sure, romance movie stuff, but there's more to it than that. Do you know about the mating ritual?"

Declan's eyes roll toward the ceiling. "Ah, jeez. I don't need to hear about weird vampire sex."

Orlando's upper lip curls. "This involves your sister, so I'd smarten up, if I were you. I can just as easily have this conversation with Colette alone. There's no need for you to be here."

Declan crosses his arms over his chest. "Go on. Vampire mating ritual. Educate us. They don't cover that in sex ed at our school."

Orlando runs his hand through his hair, looking like he would rather not be talking about any of this. "It's not well spelled out in our neighborhood, either. I don't know of any who are mated in Mayfield anymore. There was a couple a few years ago, but they passed. The mechanics are more hearsay, bordering on mythology." Orlando pinches the bridge of his nose. This is far more words than he is used to speaking in one sitting. I can tell it's taxing on him.

I move to his side, rounding the counter so I can place my palm on his shoulder. My big sweetie pie always looks like he is carrying a heavier load than most, yet he never asks for a thing in return.

I rub a soothing circle on his back. "Tell me."

Orlando keeps his gaze fixed on the table, his cheeks turning pink. "Mating is... Two vampires fall in love, and..."

This is the most awkward version of the birds and the bees I've ever heard, and I had to listen to the sheriff fumble through it when I was ten. I want to remove my hand from Orlando's back, but that somehow seems like it might make things even more uncomfortable.

Orlando clears his throat. "Sometimes they share a connection that's more intense than nature has room for. I don't know much about the transformation, but the moment it happens, the man's body and the woman's body go through this sort of... I don't know, like they're dying, but not really. It's more like the start of a rebirth. Then the guy gives her his blood. His blood is the thing that seals it. They become tied on a whole new level. Almost a psychic connection."

I have no idea why we're talking about this, or what it has to do with Orlando's mother's cookies. Still, I listen. If Orlando wants to start being more vulnerable and talking about his life, that's a good thing. I can be patient even though he makes absolutely no sense.

Orlando angles his body toward me. "When you were in the bedroom with Rome, he mentioned... he said you stopped breathing. So did he."

I freeze. "Yeah, but only for half a minute or so. Not sure what happened, but I'm okay now. There was like, a booming sound. Something snapped inside of me, and I couldn't breathe for a bit."

My brother watches us both as if we are a fascinating show about wild animals. "You stopped breathing? Isn't that the kind of thing your doctor should know about?"

"It wasn't a long enough occurrence to be a legitimate problem."

Declan motions to himself. "Fine. Isn't that the kind of thing your brother, who is a medic, should know about?"

I shoot Declan a look of sheer exasperation. "I'm fine. Orlando, I'm really okay. I didn't know you were worried about that still. It was weeks ago."

Orlando still won't look up at me. "You were freezing. Rome told me you stopped breathing. That you said you loved him while you two were... and then you stopped breathing. He was worried you two might have..." He shakes his head. "But it's impossible."

Declan's nose scrunches. "Rome was worried that my sister stopped breathing because they were... what? He thought they were in the middle of a vampire mating ritual? That's ridiculous. She's not a vampire."

Orlando rolls his eyes at Declan. "I know that. He knows that. But it got a little too real. Dating someone is hard for Rome, but it worked with you, Coco. But it's on the furthest edge of what he's capable of committing to—a secret relationship with separate homes and all that."

My mouth tightens. "He asked me if he could have a

drawer, then he freaks out because he thought some weird vampire ritual was happening that might make us closer?" I shake my head at myself. "Boy, do I know how to pick them."

Orlando rests his hand on the counter. "He freaked out because the weird vampire ritual actually did start to happen. It's not anything as temporary as dating, or even as wedding vows. It's a soul connection, a psychic link. You're tethered together in ways normal people like us can't even imagine. But the thing is, it has to be two ways. You both started the vampire mating ritual, and he needed to finish it by giving you his blood to drink."

I gape at him. "I did no such thing! I didn't mate with him. It's called making out, which is nothing as scandalous as you're making it sound. I wouldn't even know how to do something like that."

Orlando grinds his fists into his forehead. "I'm explaining it wrong. It's like some part of your being or soul or whatever wants to link itself to his. Then his soul or being or whatever has to link itself to yours. It's bigger than sex. Bigger than love, even."

Anger the likes of which I try never to feel at full volume flares up inside of me. "Well, isn't that fantastic? I put myself out there, and he ran. Awesome. I don't know why we have to talk about it, or how you know more about my body and my breakup than I do. Oh, probably because he told you what happened before he ran out on me. Must be nice. I got to be afraid that I couldn't breathe, smack in the middle of my boyfriend running out on me with no explanation. Screw him! And screw you, Orlando, for keeping this from me for weeks now. You realize I had nothing to do with any of this. I'm not a vampire! Whatever you're thinking my being or my soul did, it didn't. I'm human. I should think that logic would be obvious to you both."

Orlando lowers his head like a scolded pup.

"And I thought I told you both not to talk about him or say his name in front of me. This is exactly the kind of conversation I don't want to have." I stomp towards the front door. "I need some air. When I come back, I don't want to talk about this from now until the end of eternity."

Orlando stands, surprising me by following after me. "You were freezing," he explains, once again not making a lick of sense. "You were icy to the touch no matter how many layers you had on, or how hot I cranked the thermostat. You lost your sense of taste. You weren't sleeping."

"That last one is typical of every breakup ever. And the first one is typical of most smaller women when winter is on the way. What's your point?"

"Your soul needs its mate. You started the ritual. Your body is off because Rome didn't complete it."

My upper lip curls. "My body is amazing, and none of your business, thank you very much." I grab my coat and punch my arms into the sleeves. "My soul and my body don't need any man for anything ever!"

"Your hat," Orlando reminds me, reaching to the top shelf of the closet to grab down a knitted cap. Trouble is still brewing behind his eyes as more of his confession bubbles out. "I didn't mean to mess with the mating ritual. You were freezing. Your teeth were chattering. You wandered through the halls at night like a zombie, and I knew Rome wasn't coming back."

"Do not say his name in my house! Do you think I want to talk about this with you?!" I shout, fisting the knob and throwing the door open. I march out into the cold, regretting this choice in the first few steps. It's bitter out, and I've been having a hard time holding onto heat.

Which proves nothing, other than that it is winter. Obviously.

Orlando shuffles out onto the walkway a step behind me, unwilling to let me stomp off in a rage. "I was trying to help, so I went out on a limb to test a theory. Maybe you didn't need Rome's blood to settle your body. Maybe it was just any vampire's blood. Or a vampire's blood that was genetically similar to Ro..." He flinches at saying the name I have forbidden. "Maybe you needed blood that was similar to Mister Valentino's."

My steps slow as his words hit me like a ton of bricks.

Declan trots behind us, unwilling to let this story end partway through. "What did you do, Orlando?"

His eyes close as he stops walking. He waits for me to turn toward him before he speaks. "There's a reason my tea calms you down and helps you sleep. Your body was trying to mate with... with Mister Valentino. It was in crisis when he left the ritual undone. I thought..." Orlando rubs the nape of his neck. "I thought it would bind you two together so you could get some sleep."

"Do you think I want to be bound to a selfish baby who runs out on me when I'm choking to death?!" I can't stop screeching my ire. "You had no right to tie me to him. He didn't want that, and neither do I!" I stop myself and shake my head, willing sense to come back into my brain. "None of this is possible, Orlando. I'm not a vampire! I kill vampires, remember?"

Declan's nose scrunches. "This is beyond insane, Orlando. You're the sensible one."

Orlando hugs himself around the middle. "My cousin will come back. He panicked, is all. I don't want you to be dead from hypothermia before he comes to his senses. But it didn't work. Or it didn't work how I thought it would. I've been putting a few drops of my blood into your tea, Coco. I hoped if you drank my blood, it would tether you to him, but that's not what happened."

I am shivering, but I'm not sure that's what has set my lower lip quivering. "What, then? What happened?"

Orlando's voice quiets. "You had the urge to bake oatmeal raisin cookies with caramel popcorn in them. My mother's recipe. You said yourself that you didn't know how to make caramel corn. You just guessed and it turned out."

I rest my fist on my hip. "I cannot follow your ADD today, Orlando. What are you trying to say?"

I can see very little from the front porch light's glow, but the shadows under Orlando's eyes are clear as day. "Today is the anniversary of my mother's death."

All fight leaves me in a gust, pushing me toward him. "What? Oh, honey. I'm sorry. I didn't know." My hand rests on his arm, putting aside my irritation with him because that is not as important as his grief.

Declan swears, though it doesn't sound like regret; it's more like Declan stumbled into a revelation that thus far, has eluded me. "You don't think..."

"What?" I look from Declan to Orlando, but neither of them seems to want to fill in the blanks for me.

Orlando covers my hand on his arm with his palm, holding me fast to him. "My blood didn't mate you with Rome." He swallows hard and stares into my eyes with meaningful regret and worry. "I'm fairly certain that my blood finished the mating ritual, but it didn't bond you with my cousin. It bonded you to me."

22

ORLANDO'S BLOOD
COLETTE

The sound of the wind zipping by us fails to register. The rustling of the grass seems miles away. The whole of nature itself fades from my awareness. My mind goes silent, unable to accept or process the biggest curveball I never could have predicted. "I didn't..."

Orlando gives my hand a squeeze. "You're freezing. You need more blood, or you'll start to ice over again. Let's get you inside. You can hate me from in there just as well as you can out here."

"Wait. Nobody moves before I get this straight." Declan needs clarification just as much as I do. Though, I'm guessing no matter how many times we hear it, the world still won't make any sense. "Colette and Ro... Mister Valentino... were supposed to mate, but he split before he could do his part. The ritual was half-done, and it was starting to mess with Coco's body."

"That's right." Orlando seems relieved that we are starting to understand.

Declan shoves his hands into the pockets of his jacket as the wind whips by us. He shivers as he speaks. "Colette's body started freaking out because it needs his blood."

Orlando exhales, his shoulders lowering. "Yes. Mated females drink regularly from their males. Every day."

I want to throw up. I want to run away. I want to never have heard of any of this, so I don't have to deal with it.

Declan is more studious than I am. I want no additional information, but my brother needs to understand it all. "You figured that your cousin's blood and yours can't be all that dissimilar, so you put some of your blood in Coco's tea. Did it work? Did her body calm down?"

Orlando nods emphatically. "Yes, but she needs it every night. She sleeps now. She's not cold to the touch anymore if she drinks regularly."

I can't believe I'm adding to this madness, but my mouth opens, and the truth spills out. "I don't get the shakes anymore. Not since you started making that tea for me. Even with the stress of dealing with the mayor and all of that, I'm steady as ever."

Declan is instantly all about this insane plan. "Wait, this mating thing can heal my sister? It can take away the things that were wrong prior to being mated?"

Orlando shrugs. "I think so. It's all conjecture, remember. Stories passed down. But yeah. They don't get sick as easily if the female feeds regularly from the male. They strengthen each other. They know things about each other without being told." He casts me a culpable look. "Like how you knew you needed to make those cookies without knowing the recipe, the significance, or that it's the anniversary of my mother's death." He hangs his head. "I didn't mean to mate with you. This all went horribly wrong. I'm sorry, Coco. I would never…"

I don't know what to say to any of this. "You don't want to… I mean, you're not in love with…"

Orlando blanches, for which I am grateful. "No. You're perfectly… whatever, but no. You're a decade younger than me, for goodness sakes."

I frown up at him. "Hey, your cousin is ten years older than me, too. It's not that weird."

Orlando shoots me a wry look, but still doesn't let go of my hand, nor do I remove my fingers from his arm. "Do you want me to be in love with you?"

"No, but don't say it like having feelings for the likes of me is something that makes a man want to barf."

"Apologies. No. I don't like you like that. Obviously. I was only trying to help. I clean up after my family all the time. I thought this was just me doing that. Now I don't know how to undo it."

"Well, I could always just stop drinking your blood."

"It's not something that can be undone. You'll deteriorate." Orlando clears his throat. "You need my blood now. It's a medicine you'll never be able to survive without."

I mumble out an incredulous stream of cussing that makes even Declan grimace. "Are you serious?"

Orlando squeezes my hand. "Let's get you inside. You're going to freeze out here."

"Don't say it like that!"

"Like what?"

I slide my hand away from his and take a step back. "Like I'm your little woman and you need to tell me how cold I am! I'm not yours. I'm not anybody's! I don't need you to intervene. You shouldn't have dosed me with your blood, Orlando! That's a thing a girl should know is in her tea before she drinks it!" I tap my throat. "And now my throat hurts! That tea is the only thing I want, but it means that we're..."

Orlando tucks his hands behind his back, standing at attention to absorb the brunt of my wrath. He looks like he is preparing to go before a firing squad. "I made the wrong call."

"The wrong call should get a person lost on the freeway. This is... Is this a life sentence?!"

My words cut Orlando. I can tell by the way he flinches. Still, he composes himself, remaining calm while I turn shrill, giving my terror a voice. "There's no undoing it. None that I know of, at least. And I could be wrong."

I blink up at him. "Are you?"

"No."

I throw my head back. "Then don't get my hopes up! Now what? Do we have to live together?"

"No. We don't have to do anything, other than I need to give you my blood every day, and you need to drink it. Other than that, we can have totally separate lives."

"Then that's what we should do. Declan, can you take over watching the house?"

My brother steps toward me. "Of course. Fintan, the sheriff and I can rotate."

I bite back my groan of having to deal with Fintan on a regular basis. "Good. Orlando, I think my family can take it from here. Thanks for watching out for me these past few weeks, but this is too much. We can meet up once a day to do the blood thing, but other than that, we shouldn't... I don't want this to become something that takes over our lives."

Orlando's jaw ticks, but he doesn't argue. Still, I can feel his silent displeasure. He doesn't like this idea, but he can't exactly tell me what to do, being that he is the reason we are mired in this mess. "Whatever you like. Now can we go inside? You're freezing."

I ball my fists, my voice turning shrill. "Don't tell me how cold I am!"

Orlando inhales his frustration. "Fine. *I'm* freezing. Can we go inside because *I'm* cold?"

"Oh, fine." I stomp past him, keeping up my anger, but

part of me is already planning on throwing the blanket over his shoulders the second we get back inside.

Do I want to take care of him, or is the mate bond compelling my steps?

No, I love my big sweetie pie. Not in this exact moment, sure, but on a normal day, of course I would get him a blanket if he was cold.

Declan and Orlando murmur to each other, but I want no part of it. I step into my home, fighting off a shiver. I pick up the thick blanket on the arm of the couch. Though I'm so mad, I can hardly work out intelligible sentences, I drape the blanket around Orlando.

Then I turn on my heel and march to my bedroom, wondering how on earth I can undo this chaos.

The guys leave me alone until a quiet knock interrupts my stuttering thoughts.

Orlando pops open my door and stands in the entrance, his chin lowered in submission. "You need to drink this. Then I'll get out of your space. Declan's staying here tonight."

I hate that the scent of the tea jerks my senses to the forefront.

I don't say a word, even as my lower lip quivers. I don't want this to be real, but when the first gulp trickles down my throat, there is no denying the truth.

My body needs Orlando's blood—whether I like it or not.

23

BREAKFAST AND DINNER

COLETTE

My hair is being a problem this morning, so it ends up in a high bun atop my head.

Am I worried about being partially mated to Orlando, of all people? Of course. Can I stand to touch those feelings with a ten-foot pole? Not a chance. We have been avoiding each other since the wretched truth came to light.

Though, he still lives here. I can't even call it staying here. Orlando lives here now. He doesn't have a drawer, like his cousin wanted. We had a whole stinking dresser moved into the spare bedroom.

Did I want Orlando to move in? No. I believe I said that quite clearly. But it turns out that being far away from your mated person is problematic. The little psychic nuances aren't mere suggestions; they are compulsions. If Orlando's back hurts, my palms literally itch until I've fetched him a heating pad.

We learned that the hard way, when I turned up on his doorstep at four in the morning with a heating pad earlier this week.

That had been hard to explain when Nico was the one who answered the door. Luckily, I didn't have to tell him much, only that Orlando needed some documents that I had. That sent Nico back to his bed without further questions.

After that, Orlando and I agreed that he would move in with me under the guise of being my nighttime guard.

There's not a thing about this I don't hate, but it's something I need to make my peace with, or I will make us both miserable.

When I move down the hallway of my home, the scent of bacon greets me.

Perhaps having Orlando here isn't entirely terrible.

"You didn't have to make breakfast," I chide him, reaching for the glass of juice he has ready for me. I don't know what to do with this sort of consideration. I have to remind myself that neither of us are doing anything other than acting on the normal soul bond that happens in these types of situations.

Orlando is seated at the counter in the tall stool, his eyes on the newspaper while he munches on a piece of rye toast—my favorite. "You're low on iron."

My mouth pops open. I almost ask him how on earth he would know something like that when I don't even know it, but my jaw snaps shut when the answer becomes obvious.

Orlando knows what I need. It feels icky that he knows what I need before I do. I'm sure many people would love to have a connection like that, but in their imaginations, those people probably want to be in love with said person. Right now, it just feels like an intrusion on my privacy.

Another crutch I will never be able to survive without.

Though, if this new life comes with bacon, I'm not sure I should be complaining.

I fix myself a plate, smearing butter on my toast. "This is really fantastic, Orlando. Thank you."

My big sweetie pie grunts in response. I know he hates this arrangement, too, but he's too much a grownup to say so.

"Hey," I say to him, bringing him out of his cloud of isolation. Just because we're both unhappy doesn't mean we have to make each other pay for it. I wait for his gaze to connect with mine before I speak. "I really am grateful. I know you sort of have to do what the compulsions tell you to, but I'm still grateful. This is really nice. I think the last person to make breakfast for me was Declan, back when I lived at home."

Other than my nurse, but I don't count that.

Orlando takes my appreciation in stride, nodding at my words. I can tell a small veil between us has been lifted.

Though there are many layers of dysfunction, at least one of them is gone now.

And just like that, a new precedent has been set; even though we are compelled to act on our urges, we are going to pretend that the other person is just downright thoughtful to do so.

"It's no trouble. I haven't made bacon in a while." He turns his eyes back to his newspaper. "I like the spitting and crackling noise it makes."

Cooking the bacon wasn't really his choice, but sharing that small tidbit of his personality with me was one hundred percent his desire.

It would never occur to me that the stoic Orlando would want to be known, but I guess this morning is filled with surprises.

"Oh, yeah? I'm always afraid I'll burn it or burn myself, so I never cook it."

He makes a concerted effort to keep his face from mine. Like even though he's tearing down a small wall, he feels the need to put up another to protect himself. "When I cook it myself, I'm around the smell for a long time. Then when I sit down, I find that I eat less of it, because I've been around the smell longer."

The corner of my mouth lifts. "Like curing hunger by osmosis. That's smart."

The compliment is too much for him, so he buries his nose deeper in the paper.

I take my time savoring the spread. Though this isn't how I thought my life might turn out, in this moment, I can't complain.

Or, I can, but my mouth is stuffed with bacon.

Thoughts of Mister Valentino pop into my mind, but I am getting better at batting them back into their box, where they never see the light of day. At one point, I daydreamed about sharing mornings like this with him, but that seems like a lifetime ago. Though it's been just over a month since he split, melancholy still finds me. But then the sadness is quickly replaced with self-loathing, because I cannot believe I let myself carry on like that over a man who turned out to be essentially a grown toddler.

I don't like being alone with my thoughts these days, so I snatch my earbuds off the counter and put them in. Orlando doesn't like noise in the morning, and I like loud, incoherent metal to drown out my sadness. It must be chaotic enough to be barely able to be classified as music.

Otherwise I can hear my thoughts, which is unacceptable.

I'm just about finished with my meal when Orlando taps me on the shoulder, and then taps his ear.

I turn off my music and forget to adjust the volume of my voice. "What's up?" I shout by mistake.

Orlando smirks and then points at my phone that's resting beside the fridge. "Your phone is ringing."

"Oh. Whoops." I move across the kitchen to answer it.

"Sheriff? What's wrong?" It's not exactly "hello," but my father never calls me unless something bad happened and I need to stay inside, or perhaps if he's mad at me.

"Hi, Coco. Good morning. How are you?"

My father sounds like he's reading from a script. "What?"

"How are you?"

I examine his question, certain I'm not understanding what he truly means to be asking. "I'm safe. Why? What's wrong?"

"Nothing. I didn't call to report any crimes in your area. I just wanted to say good morning to my daughter. Is that so strange?"

I pull the phone back and stare at the caller ID to make sure I am seeing things correctly. "Uh, yeah. To be honest, it's a little strange. Is something wrong?"

The sheriff sighs. "No. I really did just call to say good morning. I guess I'm out of practice."

Understatement. I can't remember the last time my father wished me a good morning, if ever. "Okay. Good morning, then. Now will you tell me why you really called?"

I can hear the frustrated huffs on his end. "Is it a crime for me to call my daughter for no reason?"

"Not a crime, but it's not like you. Okay, um. Hi. I'm doing well. Getting ready for work right now. Just finishing up breakfast."

"What are you eating?"

I don't know why telling my dad the meal seems like I am confessing to a crime. He doesn't know that Orlando cooked. "I'm having bacon, juice and toast."

"All you're missing is scrambled eggs. I had oatmeal this morning."

"With raisins and cinnamon?"

"You know it. No point in messing with perfection."

"One day, you could try putting brown sugar in, you know."

"Sugar in the morning makes my teeth hurt."

I laugh through my nose because I knew he would say that. This is so normal a conversation that it feels alien, but I keep up with it, because it's important to my father for some reason that I still cannot decode. "You heading in to the precinct soon?"

"Just putting my shoes on."

"Hey, thanks for moving your meetings with the Valentinos. Nothing personal, it just wasn't good for business."

"That's fine, Coco. It was an experiment. Though, I've got to be honest, meeting with Nico last time was a bust. He's not built for leadership."

Understatement. "Sounds about right."

"I'm seeing Rome today at a restaurant in Midtown, which works just fine for me."

My blood freezes in my veins. "You're not meeting with Nico?"

"Nico's a good kid, but he's still a kid. Rome and I will be making plans like usual while Orlando stands guard."

My breakfast threatens to make a reappearance. "Oh," is the most I can manage.

Mister Valentino is in Mayfield? He's been in Mayfield for how long? I thought he left town. Orlando told me he left town, and so did my ex the moment he became my ex. No one told me he'd returned.

My knees turn to jelly, making it a gamble as to whether or not they want to continue holding me upright.

Mister Valentino has been close enough to come back and set things right, but he choose to leave them broken.

Because we are broken up.

"Coco?" my father says, his voice louder.

"Yeah?" My croak is the most I can offer.

"Oh, good. I thought I lost you there." My father switches my focus back to our conversation, though my stomach still feels sick. "Coco, I was wondering…"

Here it comes. His true reason for calling.

"I was thinking it might be nice to have a family dinner at my house again. You, me and your brothers, like we did a month or so ago. Who knows? If we don't kill each other, maybe we could make it a regular thing. Like, first Friday of the month I cook for everyone at my place."

I chew on my lower lip. It's the strangest thing my

father has ever asked of me because it is so painfully normal. "You want a monthly family dinner with the four of us?" I pinch the bridge of my nose. "Can I ask why? We never ate dinner together when we all lived under the same roof."

Maybe that was harsh, but it's no less true.

My father's voice comes back with a softness that is tinted with regret. "I'm hoping it's not too late for me to make that up to you all. I'm not much of a cook, but I can hold my own with a roast."

I shake my head at the whole situation, but muscle through my discomfort. "First Friday of the month? That works for me. I can bring something, if you like."

"This time, I'll do all the cooking. Think of it as my penance for not doing it when you were a kid. But after that, sure. We can all bring something. Maybe we can get to know each other through food."

My nose scrunches in confusion. "What brought this on? Have you been watching daytime talk shows or something?"

My father snorts. "You know I'm too busy to watch television. Just want to spend time with my kids, is all. That okay?"

"That…" It's weird, is what it is, but I don't say that. "That's okay. I'll be there."

"Six o'clock Friday, then."

I set my phone down, wondering if I downloaded an

app that takes the words of a gruff, angry old man and transforms them into that of a sitcom father.

I start in on the dishes because I need something to do with my hands. I want to be frustrated with Orlando for not telling me his cousin was in Mayfield, but it's not like he owes me a detailed update on his cousin's whereabouts.

"Everything okay?" Orlando asks, knowing full well it is not.

"Of course," I lie. Then I slip my earbuds back in and blast my metal almost-music as loud as I can, hoping to drown out the questions swirling in my head.

I wonder when it happened that my life became something not even I can recognize.

No sooner do I end the call does the doorbell ring through the house.

Orlando touches the hilt of the gun on his hip. "I'll get it."

I frown at his assumption that everything is chaos at first breath. "It's probably Declan. You'll scare him."

Orlando doesn't care about that. He peers through the peephole and then jerks his head back. "Did you have a meeting with Governor Mason?" he asks me in a hushed voice.

My mouth pops open. "Are you serious?" I straighten my hair, enraptured by the idea of the governor showing up at my home unannounced. I cast around the living room. "There's a glass of water on the coffee table! I haven't dusted in... Probably not since I moved in!"

Orlando's shoulders lower. "If the governor is showing up at your door unannounced, I'm guessing she has more important things on her mind than your housekeeping habits."

I hold my breath, my mind rattling through all the fathomable reasons the governor might want a private conversation with me.

Orlando waits for my nod and then opens the door, ushering in a portion of my life I never dreamed possible.

24

THE GOVERNOR'S REQUEST

COLETTE

Governor Mason is the picture of poise and power. She is dressed in a fine navy pinstriped suit that's been tailored to perfection and paired with heels that make her look formidable.

That's what I thought I was dressing like, but now that she is here and in my home for some inexplicable reason, I can see the vast cavern between my attire and hers.

I curtsey because I am a dork and unsure of myself at the moment. "Madam Governor. So nice to see you." I've only ever interacted with her in the boardroom, and she generally remains on the periphery. To have her in my house?

I don't know what to expect.

"No, it's not nice to see me under the circumstances, but I appreciate the lie. I know you've got a salon to get to, and you," she pauses to look Orlando up and down appraisingly, "must have some completely nonviolent and legal business to attend to as well. I'll make myself brief. May we sit?"

Orlando is unimpressed by humans in general, and the governor is no exception. He doesn't move to sit, nor does he offer her a seat. "You said you would make this brief. Let's hear it."

The corner of Governor Mason's mouth quirks. "I've no cause to like you, but I find I can't help myself when you pour on the charm like that. Seated is best, in case our delicate flower feels the need to faint when she hears what I have to say."

Normally anyone insinuating that I am delicate sends me in an irate tizzy filled with the need to prove the accuser wrong. But I am off my game, having her in my house like this.

"Of course." I move us toward the dining room, which thankfully only has Orlando's notes and mine atop it. The governor no doubt has little time or patience for clutter.

Orlando sits beside me, with the governor on the other side of the table. "You were right when you said we have a day to get on with. Out with whatever it is you've come here to say."

I step on Orlando's foot under the table but keep my smile in place.

She quirks a manicured eyebrow at him. "Curious that you're here at this early hour. Do you often come to

Madam Deadblood's home for breakfast, or did you stay the night?"

Orlando stiffens. "You can't be so removed from reality that you don't remember the many times Colette was abducted while living in Mayfield. Our families are friends, so I stay here sometimes to watch the house as a favor to her father and a protection for my people. If she is taken, it's the vampires who pay the price."

It's more information than Orlando wants to give her, I can tell, but he rushes through the explanation because he wants her out of here. Orlando is a private person, and doesn't like strangers in his home.

Our home.

Man, did that sneak up on me.

She feathers her fingers in front of her lips. "That's perfect. I was thinking Rome would make a stronger statement, but you'll do." She waves her hand when it's clear she isn't making a lick of sense. "I'm here because I read over your proposal for the city's budget. Splitting the budget evenly between the East and West End is a big deal, and would change a lot for not just Mayfield, but for the entire world."

I blink at her words and slide into business mode. "That's true, but it's change that's long overdue. We cannot pretend that we've given vampires a fair shot at the world when we give them table scraps and complain when they can't lift their heads."

"I quite agree."

What?

She has been silent in the meetings, her presence there more as an observer than a partaker in policy changes.

Orlando is listening now, and less insistent that she get out. "That's surprising you agree. You haven't said so in the meetings. No one else in Mayfield's government seems to be on the same page we are."

"Well, they like things safe and small. I do not. I've been waiting until I had a moment to speak privately with you before I throw my considerable weight behind your proposal. I am prepared to go to the mayor's office right now and demand he push this change through immediately. This and the education reform you submitted that's set to go through in the fall. Next school year is too long to wait for your changes."

My entire body lights up. "You are? Oh, Governor Mason, that's wonderful! It would do so much for so many people. Thank you!" I fan my face. "This whole thing has felt like it's moving so slow. To have your help speeding things along? This is exactly what we were hoping you would do."

Orlando goes still, eyeing her with caution only a Valentino can wear like a suit and tie. "What's it going to cost us?"

It's a bold question and one that sends my elation into chagrin. "Orlando, honestly. She's here because she wants to help the vampires. We have a solid plan, and she is sensible enough to recognize that. There's no other reason."

It's the first time I've ever seen the cool governor squirm. "Well, actually... Yes. This is a fantastic plan you've come up with. However, it's not enough."

"Not enough?" I grimace. "Do you think Mayor Stapleton will agree to something more? I got the feeling I was pushing him further than he can stretch."

She eyes the two of us appraisingly. "I think the goal is to make the vampires equal citizens with equal opportunity, is it not?"

My brows push together. "Well, yes. But that's a broad idea that requires a lot more change than the world will accept. One step at a time, which is what we've been working on."

While you've been pretty much silent in every meeting.

Governor Mason leans forward. "My dear, do you truly not realize how much power you hold? If you wore a shoe on your head and called it a hat, that would become the newest fashion within a week."

I snicker at her assessment. "If only. I've been trying to affect actual change for months now, and all I've gotten is a few parks renovated and a promise that the schools will adhere to a balanced budget in the fall of next year."

Her voice drops conspiratorially. "That's because you haven't hit the right pressure point. The mayor doesn't care about doing the right thing for people who can't vote him out of office. He cares about reelection. He cares about keeping his majority voters happy and sedated." She sits back and clucks her tongue. "What would the world come to if Madam Deadblood was seen out and about with a vampire man on her arm? Over time, perhaps the humans would stop viewing the vampires as dogs and start seeing them as people. As possibilities."

My nose crinkles. "Possibilities for what?" I tilt my head to the side and jerk my thumb toward Orlando. "My family has always been close with the Valentinos. It's no scandal for people to see us together in public. Maybe it still makes them uncomfortable, but they've accepted it."

Orlando shrugs. "She's right. It's no surprise for us to be seen talking. I don't understand what you're getting at."

The governor shakes her head, firm that we will not miss her point. "No, Madam Deadblood. The world evolves because your father and Joseph Valentino forced the world to step up and accept that vampires can break bread with humans. Before their friendship, people didn't realize they could hang out together. Now they can go shopping together. They can go on family vacations together." She motions between Orlando and me. "I think it's high time the world evolved once more."

I have no idea what she is talking about. "I feel like we're already doing that, and it's not destigmatizing vampires milling about in Midtown. It's not opening up the mind of the mayor to rethink the city's budget."

Governor Mason presses her painted lips together before continuing. "You're not hearing me, Madam Deadblood. It's not enough for you to be seen being friendly with the vampires. It's not a radical enough step forward because the people have grown used to it, yet still their blatant bigotry is allowed to fester."

"I don't understand what you want us to do. We're pushing this proposal for budget reform as hard as we can."

She points to me. "I've seen an untapped resource you haven't tried yet."

I glance at Orlando for an interpretation of whatever point she is trying to make, but he merely shrugs. "We're all ears."

The governor levels her gaze at me. "I've seen you in the meetings. During the first few where Rome was by your side, I couldn't look away. Rome Valentino was not afraid to touch your wrist, nor you, his. Orlando puts his arm on the back of your chair. The three of you aren't afraid to be near each other."

My face flushes. "I'm sure I don't know what you mean. They are old friends. They are like brothers to me." Bile rises in my throat just saying those words.

Mister Valentino isn't like a brother to me. He is like a

lightning bolt send straight from Hades to enrapture and destroy my heart.

The governor touches her lips. "Where is Rome? I haven't seen him in Mayfield in a while."

"He took a sabbatical, but he's back in Mayfield now," Orlando explains. "If you're trying to reach a point, you are failing."

Orlando doesn't like to speak, much less to humans who aren't me, so I know he has reached his peak frustration.

The governor straightens. "Where did Mister Valentino escape to?"

"He is in and out of town at the moment. Much to see to." Orlando doesn't answer further, but rather stares down the governor, letting her know that question is out of bounds and is none of her business.

The governor seems to understand that Orlando wants her to cut to the heart of why she is here. She presses her hands flat atop the table. "If you want this new budget pushed through, I can throw my considerable weight behind it. But what I require in return is for you to fight a bit harder for vampire-human relations to be destigmatized. I would like for it to start circulating that our Madam Deadblood has taken up with a vampire. Preferably the most notable one whom the humans already recognize. It won't do for her to be seen holding hands and fawning over some no-name vampire. I want someone the people cannot look away from." She draws a line with her nails across the length of the table. "I'd thought Rome, but Nico Valentino will do. He is certainly more age appropriate, and nearly as recognizable. If Rome is in and out of town, perhaps Nico would be a better choice."

The grimace that contorts my face is only a portion of the horror I feel at her suggestion. "You cannot be serious. No one would ever believe Nico and I could be dating."

She tilts her chin as she stares at me. "No one? I happen to think you fake happiness well enough for the viewers already. This is nothing more than holding onto your friend's hand in public and selling the lie that you two are dating."

I balk at her, doing my best to push aside the absurdity of her suggestion. Rome and I went to extremes to make sure no one found out about us. A pairing this controversial would set off a powder keg that might implode the world.

Which is exactly what Governor Mason intends to do, apparently.

I splutter at the suggestion. "Why? Why on earth would... Just why?"

The governor's demeanor softens. "Because for the government to move, it must be acting in the best interest of the people. No one sees the vampires as people, my dear. If you want the changes to happen, it cannot be at the top level only. Everyone roots for you. Everyone wants to see what you're wearing, who you're hanging out with. If you make it clear that you want to be in a relationship with a vampire, they will begin to want this for you, too. Then they won't be so opposed or surprised when we roll out this new budget for the school system." She meets my gaze with purpose. "You see, there is more to this than just the school system. If you want the world to change, sometimes you need to give it a little push. If you don't want it to break in the process, then you need to make them want this change—even if it involves trickery." She leans back in her seat. "So, my dear, I think the question I have for you is: how badly do you want the world to change? Will you tell a little lie to make it so?"

I gnaw on my lower lip, terrified of everything she is suggesting. "I don't know. Nico will never go for it, for starters. He hates me."

"He hates you more than he loves his people? I find that hard to believe."

Lady, you don't know Nico like I do.

"Will you agree if he volunteers his hand?"

I rub my forehead, vexed and perplexed that this might actually be happening.

Of course it would happen with Nico. Of course this presents itself when my boyfriend is gone from my life.

It's just as well. Mister Valentino is not strong enough to handle the vitriol that will aim itself our way when this comes to light.

I lower my head. "If Nino loves his people more than he loves his hatred of me, then sure. I'll do it. It's just holding hands and smiling at him in public, right? That's dating."

The governor grins as she sits back. "Why yes, it is. Splendid." She angles her chin toward Orlando. "Would you like me to stop over in the West End to ask Nico to do this, or would that be best coming from you?"

Orlando stands. "I will speak to Nico about this today. Consider the Valentino family in. We will uphold our end of things. Anything to help our people."

My head hangs as Orlando escorts the governor to the door. This is not what I had in mind for my life. In fact, this is just about the worst thing I can think of to save Mayfield from its own bigotry.

But it must be done, so I will do it.

25

NICO'S HAIRCUT
COLETTE

I am less chatty this morning than usual, though far more productive. I've stepped back from actually doing salon work, per the plan for me to do more for the cause to push relations between the vampires and the humans forward. But when the salon's phone rings and my name is called over the sound of hair dryers, I realize I am nowhere near ready to step away from the business I created.

Rachel is doing a fine job of running things. We just need to hire another stylist. Unfortunately, finding a stylist who will work on both human and vampire hair is a challenge.

I know the solution: I need to hire a vampire stylist to work here.

One giant hurdle at a time.

"Kennedy Salon. This is Colette. How can I help you?"

"This is Dana from Greens and Grabs. Huh. I didn't realize the number was to the Kennedy Salon. Interesting. Is this..." The woman gasps, her tone turning awestruck. "You're Colette Kennedy."

It is the first time my constant motion ceases. It's as if the whole world slows. My preoccupation with staying busy falls to the wayside as my brain narrows in to focus.

This is me. This is something *I* wanted. Something I still want. Something I was pursuing before I let the end of a relationship wreck my plans. I sell my own shampoos and conditioners out of my salon, but I've been dreaming of turning this into a real empire. I couldn't tell Mister Valentino because he would have forced a store to buy my products in the same way he forced my landlady to lower my rent.

I can't believe the rent on my salon here in Midtown didn't shoot back up after he split.

I chew on my lower lip, nervous and excited all at once. "I am Colette Kennedy. I'm glad to hear from you, Dana."

"Well, I would have put your products on my shelf without even trying them, had I known you were the one behind them. You sent us a box of your hair care products not too long ago. I can't believe that was you."

I smile at her wonder. "That's why I didn't tell you. I wanted my products to be good enough on their own."

"Well, that's quite the twist."

My tongue sweeps across my lower lip. "What did you think of the samples I sent?"

I know my products work. I know they are good because I use quality ingredients with no sodium lauryl sulfate (no sulfates of any kind, actually), and no fillers. I make them with my own hands and use them myself.

But it doesn't matter if I like them. I've learned that in this business, it doesn't even matter if they work. You need a killer marketing strategy and visibility.

I don't have to worry much about visibility. I am fairly certain I could have opened a shop that sold only old newspapers, and people would still want to come in and see the Last Deadblood from Mayfield. It's the pricing I'm worried about. I priced myself sustainably, even factoring in that I might need to eventually hire someone to make the products if it takes off.

Usually pricing yourself sustainably is the thing that gets you booted out of the market.

I hold my breath until Dana answers.

"I love the shampoo. My hair has never been healthier. I want to sell your products in our store. We're not the biggest, but if you want a spot on our shelves, the numbers you sent in the package as far as cost per unit will work for us."

I don't know what this feeling is. It's not hope. It's not happiness, exactly. It's like a balloon is expanding in my chest, lifting me to a mindset I didn't realize existed five minutes ago. "That's fantastic. Thank you, Dana. Thank you for trying them. Thank you for this opportunity." I close my mouth before I start gushing.

"Let's start with a hundred units. I'll reorder when I have twenty percent left. New products get featured on the endcap for two weeks. You'll need to send over any materials you want featured there."

"Yes. Absolutely." I have none of those things, but that hardly matters. A store said yes. They want me because I made something useful. I'm not just a name. I create things.

Things people want to buy.

When the call ends, I feel as if I am floating.

I did it. My brand is expanding.

I move through the store without a trace of weight on my shoulders. So elated am I that I don't realize that the atmosphere in the salon has shifted until Rachel calls my name. "Colette, do you want to take this one?"

I turn, surprised because I am only on the schedule to do admin today, not cut hair. But when I see who it is, I understand. "Hi, Nino-bear. What can I do for you and your friends?"

If he's here to start trouble, so help me...

"You can call me Nico, for starters. Orlando came by and explained things to me." The youngest Valentino looks angry that he is here in my salon with countless human women gaping at him warily. His feet are shoulder-width apart, like he's gearing up to take a punch. His fists clench in time with his jaw tightening. He's got two of his men flanking him. "We're supposed to get our hair cut here. Orlando's orders." He glances to the clientele who are entirely human. Then he lowers his voice, approaching me so our conversation isn't had at a shout. "Making a statement to the city and whatnot that we're all one big happy family." He looks like he's about to choke on his own rage. "Is this believable?"

I lean in to whisper to him. "That you're standing here waiting for a haircut or that we're dating? Because honestly, that's a no on both fronts."

Nico exhales his frustration. "This is a stupid idea."

"Granted." At least we agree on that. "Take a seat," I say to the lackey on the left. "You want highlights, right?"

The vampire's upper lip curls so he can show off his fangs.

Little does he know that display does nothing to intimidate me. What's he going to do? Bite me and kill himself in the process? Give me a break.

The vampire lackey glowers at me. "Let's get this over with as quick as possible."

"My sentiments exactly." I motion to the very first chair in the row, which is the one I always use. "Which one are you? Thing One or Thing Two?"

"Just cut my hair."

"Well, when you ask so nicely." I fan out the lavender

bib and fasten it at his nape, noting that yes, he does need a haircut. The Valentinos rarely allow anything resembling sloppiness, even in their traveling muscle. I can tell they were supposed to come here a while ago but put it off until they were sent probably with some sort of threat.

I don't ask the man what he wants. I don't even care to ask his name. This is a formality, a statement, and nothing more.

I get out the clippers and trim up the back and sides, then feather my scissors through the top to give him a bit more texture to the hair that stands atop his head. I would normally wash the gel out before I start a cut, but for obvious reasons, I rush through.

Though the music playing through the salon is sultry and sweet, there is no pep or merriment anywhere in sight. Everyone either getting their hair cut or waiting for their turn is watching my every movement to see the oddity that is a vampire in a human business. There are several businesses all through Midtown that have signs reading *"Humans Only"* in their windows. Most, in fact. Though mine welcomes both, it is a rare occurrence for vampires to actually take me up on the offer.

I lean in to speak quietly to the vampire. "The whole reason you're here is to make a statement. You're supposed to be showing the humans that you're not scary to be around, and that you have every right to be here. But right now, you look like you're one bad haircut away from shooting up the place. You *want* to be here, remember? You belong here as much as anyone else. Start acting like it."

He snarls, meeting my eyes in the mirror. "How? I don't want to be here."

"Try smiling."

He scoffs. "Be serious."

"Try anything other than scowling. This isn't worth your time or mine if you can't put on a believable show. See? I can do it, too." I pause to let out a tinkling laugh, as if he's just said something entertaining.

"Just finish so we can get out of here."

I point to the mirror. "You're nervous. Just look at yourself. Don't look at anyone else. They don't matter. Right now, it's just you and me." I point to the mirror until he complies, his rounded cheeks firm with frustration. "Good. Now look at yourself and tell me if this feels right."

He seems to drop his attitude for a moment and truly consider my query. "It can stay a bit longer on top, maybe. What do you think?"

I soften at his curiosity. "I think that would look nice. Still clean around the sides and back, but a bit more personality on top. Can I show you something you might like?"

"I guess."

After I finish with the cut, I take a round brush and

blow dry the front so that his hair stands up instead of falling limply onto his forehead. "Handsome, right?"

He stares at his reflection, his mouth pulling to the side. "I mean, not ugly, that's for sure."

"You know I'm not settling for a lousy 'not ugly.' You can do better than that for a look this sharp."

Victor's chair is beside mine, but he has been mute this entire time. Finally, he straightens the brunette bun atop his head and chimes in with a boisterous, "Honey, you're not leaving here until you tell the world that you're a handsome devil."

The vampire guard's neck shrinks. "I'm not saying that."

"You most certainly are, and loud enough for the people gaping at you to hear."

He grins, the tips of his ears turning pink. "Fine, fine. I'm a handsome devil."

"Louder!" Victor cheers, clapping twice.

He stands and tears off his bib, spikes it like a football and throws his arms up in the air with a grin that shows off his fangs. "I'm a handsome devil!"

Rachel hoots and hollers, and a few other people in the waiting area clap for fear of not agreeing with the terrifying clientele. Still, they're spreading positivity, however forced.

I'll take it.

I cut the second vampire's hair in much the same fashion, and he too is treated to applause from the salon.

We need to make this a thing. People come in here to feel better about themselves. If I was applauded, I would remember that haircut. I would come back. I would feel special and cute for an entire day.

That's what I want to create in here. I want an experience, not just a service.

Nico is less cheery, but I get through his haircut without garroting him, so I figure that's a win all the way around.

"This doesn't change anything," Nico warns me as I brush off his freshly shaven nape. "I still think you're stupid for opening up a salon here. You belong in the East End. You're like, their queen. A symbol for every ignoramus who hates vampires just for existing." He shakes his head. "I don't care what Orlando wants. I can't do this." He motions between the two of us. "No. No and never."

All chances of cheer leave my lungs in a gust. "I don't hate you. I love you, even when you're being mean like this." Though we're supposed to be putting on a show, I pledge those words with utmost sincerity.

Hurt flickers across Nico's eyes. "If you love me, then you won't carry on like this. You won't force me to look at you." He stands, tears off his bib and throws it on the floor.

Several people step back from Nico, even though they've been giving him a wide berth.

The salon is silent, but for the buzzing of clippers as Nico spits on my shoe. He points at my face as I fight for composure. "Every time I look at you, all I see are the vampires who died because of your blood. It's you who killed my father. You know that, right? He was shot with a bullet dipped in your blood."

A ripple of gasps fan out across my business. I'm guessing Orlando forced Nico to pretend to date me instead of reasoning with him. That never goes well with Nico, who is more bullheaded than most.

The verbal lashing stings. It is widely known in Mayfield that Daddy Valentino died because of my blood. It is also well known that our families were closer than close growing up. That my blood was used to murder the man I called "Daddy" is a tragedy for which I still have not forgiven myself. But when Nico lays it out so succinctly, the scandal is relived all over again.

My private shame is fodder for public scrutiny.

The knife I stab myself with when I am down digs itself deeper into my chest. It's a wound that I know will never heal.

And Nico will never let me forget it.

Nico snarls at me. Now that he is the biggest man here, he gives himself free rein to say whatever he pleases, as if being a Valentino excuses you from having to be considerate. "Rome might want to play nice, but he's forgotten himself. Forgot where he came from. Orlando sending me here?" He motions around my salon, which is still silent. "This was a mistake."

I will tolerate a lot of things, and I am definitely not my ex boyfriend's biggest fan right now, but speaking against him openly is not something a vampire should ever do. Mister Valentino is a rat bastard for leaving me like he did, but he is a saint for all he's done to help the West End. I will not have Nico undo all he has worked for just because Nico feels like being a brat.

A sneer tugs at the corner of my upper lip. My words come out in a quiet seethe, but they carry across the breadth of the salon. "How dare you. Your brother brought respect back to your people. He is the reason the vampires can hold their heads high. Do not disrespect the head of the Valentino family to me. I will not tolerate such foolishness in my place of business."

Something catches in my periphery. One of my clients is recording this entire exchange on her phone.

Make that two people.

Four.

Seven.

I cringe at the bad press. Not for my business, but for the backwards step this will be for all vampires when it gets out that Nico came in just to cause trouble.

I need to end this now.

"You should go, Nico."

I lean down to pick up the discarded bib from the floor.

I do not expect Nico's shoe to swing out.

His foot connects with my jaw, knocking a scream from my lips. My breath leaves my lungs as my head snaps back. The kick blows me off-balance and sends the salon swirling in a fit of chaos.

Nico bends over and punches me across the face. Stars pop behind my eyes as pain shoots through my cheekbone and roars through my veins.

Nico knows I won't fight back because I love him. Because the cause matters more than this fight.

Because my heart is too broken to raise my fist in my defense.

Rachel and Victor rush to my side as pain explodes over my face and humiliation washes through my insides.

A flurry of bills rains down on my head as Nino turns to his lackeys. "Listen good, everyone. We don't want to do business with any of you. I'd rather not shake hands with the people who look down their noses at us. Enjoy your privileged lives and leave us alone. We don't need your pity or your acceptance."

And with that, Nico and his lackeys exit my business, leaving me on my knees and pushing our progress back by miles.

26

BROKEN BROTHER, BRUISED SISTER

COLETTE

It was a mistake to hole up in my office after Nico kicked me in the jaw and punched me across the face. I should have driven home first thing, but I wasn't exactly walking straight. Every minute that ticks by, more and more people file into the salon, buzzing to exchange the gossip of a risk gone horribly wrong. There are reporters in my business, making it nearly impossible for my people to do their jobs.

To their credit, my stylists stonewall any questions aimed at them about the incident, and one of them comes in to check on me every twenty minutes or so.

I can't leave because the left side of my face has started to swell. That's all the bigots need is a picture of me looking beaten and forlorn for them to go off on the entire vampiric population. As if all vampires carry Nico's rage.

As if we haven't earned their disgust.

I use the time sequestered in my office to look over the contract Dana emailed over, but the numbers start to run together in my mind.

I can't focus. I can't think. All I can do is feel. My face hurts, even an hour after Nico's shoe connected with my jaw. But worse than that is the ache in my heart I try never to acknowledge.

I was the only girl in both families. I was Daddy Valentino's little princess. He would carry me on his shoulders and play hide-and-seek for as long as I wanted. The fact that my blood was used to end his life is a tragedy I still carry around my neck like a talisman of doom.

I don't blame Nico for hating me. But I wish he would have done so in private. Now the humans are going to use this as another reason to fear or hate the vampires, as if they needed permission for such things. They *want* to hate. They *want* to feel superior. Now they have this incident which will prove to them that they were right all along to keep the vampires sequestered to the West End.

If the vampires are out of sight, then we can make them out to be whatever kind of monsters we like.

I wanted to bring vampires back into East Enders' lives so they could see how much of the fear they had made up in their minds.

Now that's shot.

When a knock sounds at the door, I try to keep my voice steady. "I'm not available."

Declan's voice nearly breaks my heart. "It's me, Coco. Let me in."

"Just you?"

"Just me."

I cannot believe how steady my hand is as I unlock the door for Declan. Usually something like this would max out my nerves and set my body trembling. I'm upset, to be sure, but my body is reacting like a normal person's.

That is my one piece of sanity I have clung to over the past few hours.

My second piece of sanity enters and quickly locks the door behind him.

Declan engulfs me in a tight hug. I can feel every ounce of his anxiety, so I hold him closer, resting my good cheek on his shoulder. "I saw the video," he chokes out, his voice catching. "Then I sent the video to your doctor. I know that's overstepping, but I don't care. He said I need to take you to the emergency room to make sure there isn't any swelling in your brain." Then Declan starts to cry, breaking my heart just when it finally started to mend itself. "He said you would probably be unconscious when I got here. He warned me that you might not be able to walk, even if I got you to wake up. That your speech would be slurred if you were able to speak at all."

Now I'm the one giving the comfort while my brother falls apart in my arms. "No, no. Declan, I'm totally fine. My cheek and my jaw hurt, but I think that's par for the course when you've been kicked and punched in the head."

"I couldn't believe what I saw. Nico's lost his mind. Orlando will handle him, that is if the sheriff and Fintan don't deal with him first."

"I don't want any of that."

"I know, Coco. You want none of this to have happened in the first place. I saw your face. You were so composed. I've never been more scared, proud and furious at the same time. I want to get you out of Mayfield, but I know that's not your plan." Declan squeezes me as if he is afraid to let go as he whispers, "I wish that was your plan."

"Me too," I admit, though I hate myself for the moment of raw honesty.

"Let's get you to the emergency room. We can leave your car here for now. Lucas and I can bring it back to you later."

"Lucas?"

"He's got my car waiting for us. There are quite a few cameras camped out by your car."

I cringe. "I can't stand this whole thing."

"You up for a quick exit?"

"All I heard was 'exit'."

"Don't let go of my arm, okay? Do you have a hat to hide your face?"

"They know it's me."

"Sure, but they don't need to see how swollen your cheek is, or that your eye is starting to pop out."

I wince, wishing that I'd called in sick today. I grab a file folder and cover the left side of my face with it. "This is the best I can do."

The second the door to my office opens, the dull roar of the salon erupts with exclamations and questions all aimed my way. Rachel and Victor do what they can to shove the reporters out of our way so we can walk.

It takes some doing, but Declan manages to elbow us a path through the salon, straight out the front door. Our footsteps speed up to a run when a car's horn signals us over.

Declan opens the back door and drags me inside. I barely get the door shut before Lucas takes off, driving us away from my salon.

27

THE DANGER OF DOCTORS
COLETTE

"Kicked in the jaw and punched across the face," I tell the doctor again. It's the fourth doctor they've brought in to look at me. Not to sound all paranoid, but I'm pretty sure no one else gets this type of attention. My doctor lives overseas, so I can't just pop over to his office. Having me in the hospital here in Mayfield is akin to having an alien come to visit.

Everyone wants a crack at diagnosing me.

Though it was Declan's idea to take me in, I can tell by the disdain on his face that he regrets this choice. His arms are crossed over his chest. "You can clearly see by the MRI that there's no swelling of the brain. Is there a reason we're being kept here for a fourth opinion?"

The doctor quirks an eyebrow at my brother. "Would you prefer I take shortcuts with the Last Deadblood? Is that your professional opinion, *Emergency Medical Technician* Kennedy?"

I bristle and pop off the table, because of course we were admitted to the hospital and not merely kept in the emergency room. "Out you go. I'm finished. I was a good sport sitting through the first three examinations because those doctors were at least civil. You don't get to lord your position or your education over my brother. Not while I'm around. So unless you've found a way to clone me so there are two Deadbloods you can examine, I'm through."

The doctor stammers through his reply. "Well, I wasn't saying... I haven't finished with my evaluation. We need to do a blood draw."

Declan's jaw ticks. "Under what medical circumstance does a black eye require a blood draw? In your professional opinion, explain yourself." Declan takes out his phone. "You know what, I don't need your excuses. The sheriff is going to hear about this. Him and the fifty reporters waiting in the lobby and in the parking lot to get a look at the Last Deadblood. After we tear you apart in court for trying to take my sister's blood unduly, you'll be lucky if they let you work as something as lowly as an emergency medical technician."

My chin lifts in defiance. "Hope you weren't attached to that white coat, Doctor."

The doctor jots a few notes down, though I can tell he is panicking. "I think we can get you checked out. Ice on your eye. If you get dizzy, call an ambulance. Due to her prior head trauma, she should follow up with her primary care physician. Her eyes are still having trouble focusing, so no driving for twenty-four hours."

"Got it." Declan glares at the doctor. "Your name is going on the list of potential dangers to my sister that the sheriff keeps."

"Is that some sort of a threat?"

Declan's upper lip curls as he gets in the doctor's face. "If she doesn't get to sleep at night because of people like you gunning for her blood, then you shouldn't sleep soundly, either. Fair's fair." My brother takes a step back and points to the door. "You heard my sister. Out you go. She's finished with the exam and wants to go home."

The doctor marches out of the room, huffing his indignation that his mischief has been called out.

"Thank you," I tell my brother. "Let me get dressed and then we can get out of here."

Declan kisses my forehead because it softens us both. He's happier when he's silly. He isn't like Fintan or our father, happy only when he is in charge and intimidating people. "I'll be right outside the door. No one's taking your blood, okay?"

I nod, but the fear of that is never gone. I get myself dressed as quick as I can, though my aim is off because my eye has swollen shut. I wish I was steadier on my feet, but I count it a win because I don't fall over.

Declan offers his arm when I emerge from the room. "Lucas is meeting us at the entrance for expectant mothers. There aren't any reporters over there, but it's a bit of a hike. Are you up for it?"

"I don't know what all the fuss has been about. I could run a marathon, I'm so fine." It's a blatant lie, but neither of us care to correct me on it.

I keep my head down, my hair loose from its previous high bun so it covers as much of my face as possible. We take a few wrong turns, but fifteen minutes later, we make it to the proper exit without a trail of reporters behind us.

Declan helps me into the backseat of Lucas' car.

The worst part is that I actually do need the help. He sits beside me in the back, even though his boyfriend is up front. I feel bad that I'm being so high maintenance, but I am grateful Declan doesn't leave my side. I don't want to fall and bang my head, or do anything that might send me back to the hospital.

Lucas doesn't bother asking if I am okay as he drives us to my house. Instead, he cuts right to the heart of it. "I'm glad you're upright. How can I help?"

An exhale finds me when I thought I might have to hold my insides together forever. "This. You're driving us home. That's the best help I could ask for."

Declan quietly explains what happened with the last doctor in a slow seethe.

Lucas swears, his knuckles tightening on the steering wheel. "Did you call the sheriff?"

Declan nods. "While she was getting dressed. He's going to handle it."

"Good. I'm proud of you for calling him to ask for help with this. You did the right thing."

Though my face is still throbbing and my anxiety is sky high, gratitude washes over me that Declan found a partner who knows him well enough to say something so thoughtful. It is hard for him and me to reach out to our father to ask for help, but it was the right thing to do.

Declan reaches forward and grips the side of Lucas' seat. "I need to stay with Colette tonight."

Lucas catches my eye in the rearview mirror. "That's a good idea. Colette, would it be okay if I stayed over, too? Declan just got done working a double. I don't want him overextending himself. He can take half the night, and I'll take the other half."

The urge to tear up puts pressure behind my eyes in a way that is so painful, I grimace. "That is the sweetest thing. I love how well you look after my brother. Of course you can stay over. Today and any day. I'm sorry this is happening. It's taking over everything."

Lucas grants me a gentle smile as he turns onto the freeway. "How about you and I don't apologize to each other for things that aren't our fault. If you plan on kicking yourself in the face, then you can apologize for it. Sound good?"

"That works. You're a good person, Lucas."

"I'm in love, is what I am. Declan's sister is my sister. If my sister gets her face kicked in, I'll be there until she's back on her feet."

I touch my forehead. "Okay, you can't say anything else nice like that. It hurts to cry, and you're making me tear up with all this sweetness."

Lucas chuckles as the world whips by us. "Alright, alright."

By the time we get to my house, I am significantly calmer, though still in pain. I didn't have time to fill my prescription because that would have meant hanging around the pharmacy, which is a bad idea. So we dropped it off, deciding I would deal with the pain until the pharmacist got to my order. Then Declan can pick it up, because we've been down this road before. HIPAA rules mean precious little when it's my name that comes across the counter. The last time I had to fill something, a slew of reporters were waiting in the parking lot to bombard me with questions. So now my doctor overseas sends me my medication every month, filling it himself and sending it right to my house. It's safer that way.

Lucas parks in the garage after Declan punches in the code, and they both make a show of helping me into the house. I want to protest how over the top their care of me is, but I am dizzier than I would like to admit.

Orlando greets us from his stool at the counter. "Wonderful," he says under his breath when he sees the damage done to my face. "What took you so long to get home? I've been calling you nonstop."

I open my mouth to tell him my phone was turned off, but my words die on my tongue when I see a suitcase sitting in my kitchen. "Why is that... Are you leaving? What happened?"

The urge to beg my formidable protector not to move out overwhelms me. Despite the pain of crying, I cannot help myself. Tears slide down the right side of my face while my left side screams at me for being such a baby.

Orlando isn't mine to keep. He's not my boyfriend. He's not my anything.

But he's my big sweetie pie.

And he is my friend. The thought of him moving out is agony I didn't realize I could or would experience.

I stumble forward, bracing myself on the counter. "Please don't go, Orlando. I know I have no right to ask you to stay. I know it's weird. I know we shouldn't live together. But I don't want you to move out. Tell me why you want to go, and I'll fix it. Please give this another chance."

Fear mingles with hurt and floods my system.

Of all the things I have lost, I cannot lose Orlando.

28

POSING

COLETTE

m I begging? Am I truly begging this oaf of a man not to leave me?

My mouth sours at how pathetic I sound.

Orlando's shoulders loosen at my panic. "I'm leaving, and so are you. I don't want you sleeping here if Nico has lost his mind. I packed you some things so you would be comfortable for a few days. However long it takes me to sort him out. I don't want his lackeys coming for you after I lay down the law. Either he will learn the lesson, or Nico will double down on his anger and aim it at you. I can't have that." He lowers his chin, gearing up for vulnerability in the presence of my brother and Lucas. "You don't want me to leave? You like having me in your space?"

I've already debased myself, so I don't hold back now. I throw myself into his arms, not caring that I am clumsy and his arms are inept at holding a woman. "I do. Orlando,

I love living with you. After this business with Nico is cleared up, you'll come back here?"

I don't know if Orlando is smiling, but his arms tighten around me, letting me know he likes this idea very much. "How about I don't move out unless you tell me to go."

I exhale into his barreled chest. "Thank you."

Orlando's hand rubs slowly up and down my back.

"Whoa," Declan says, reminding me that we have an audience. "I don't know what I just witnessed. What's weirder: my sister begging a guy to stay, or Orlando acting like a man with feelings. Did I step into some alternate reality?"

The space between Orlando's eyebrows puckers at the notion that he could be slowed down by anything so ordinary as feelings. "I don't comment on your life. Best you don't comment on mine." His telling gaze shifts between Lucas and Declan, letting them know their secret relationship isn't a secret to him. "You think I don't do background checks and surveillance on anyone who comes sniffing around her? I look out for Colette. Take the help and be grateful."

Declan looks away, nervously adjusting his collar. "I'm not ready to tell the sheriff or Fintan."

Orlando snarls. "I don't care about any of that. I care that Coco was attacked by one of my family members and no one thought to call me. I'm mated to her. The hierarchy of people who get to know when she's hurt are me and then you. Got that?" He locks eyes with Lucas, whom I can tell wishes he was far away from this conversation. "That's right. Now you know a secret about me, and I know one about you. I won't tell anyone that you've taken up with the Kennedy boy, and you don't say a word about Coco and I being mated. It was an accident. It doesn't mean we're in love. It means we're family. And it means that when she's hurt, I get the first phone call."

Lucas runs his palm from his forehead to his chin. "Not a problem. I mean, I have loads of questions, but I'm guessing this isn't the time for them."

"Finally, we're on the same page."

Declan turns his head toward his boyfriend. "Lucas, you might need to let me fill you in on all of this in the morning. This is a lot more complicated than I thought it would be."

Lucas nods to Orlando, winks at me and kisses Declan before the two promise to call each other when the dust settles.

After Lucas leaves, Declan holds up his hands in surrender. "I didn't think to call you, Orlando. I'm not sure I have your number anymore, man. Let me put it in my phone, okay?"

The two exchange phone numbers in the most awkward and borderline aggressive way I've ever seen two people do such a benign thing, but part of me feels more settled, now that we are a team.

Orlando releases me and taps the suitcase with the toe of his shoe. "I've got a place that Nico doesn't know about. You can hide out there for a few days while I set him straight."

I touch Orlando's wrist. "Don't hurt Nico, Orlando."

Orlando rolls his eyes at what he assumes is my bleeding heart. "Don't you dare try that with me. Nico busted up your face, so I get to go after his."

I shake my head, but immediately regret the rapid movement. I grip the counter to keep myself upright while the world spins.

"We're sitting down," Declan insists, leading me to the nearest stool.

"You can't hurt Nico," I insist. "It won't do anything. He doesn't respond to aggression because he *is* aggressive. It only challenges him to be a bigger bully. You need to reason with him. Get him to see what we're trying to build. Get him to *want* to help us, instead of just backing down because he's afraid of getting his butt kicked."

Orlando pinches the bridge of his nose. "Can't I just bash his face in?"

A small chuckle escapes me. "Sorry. You're going to have to do this the civil way. I have faith in you. You're my big sweetie pie; you know that?"

I don't expect Orlando's neck to shrink at the cutesy nickname. I've called him that since I was a little girl and it only served to make him roll his eyes. Now he seems to like the syrupy affection. He is completely adorable like this, but I don't mention it so as not to embarrass him further.

My head drops. "We can kiss the budget reform goodbye. This is hardly the press Governor Mason asked for."

Declan's nose scrunches. "Come again?"

I cast the barest of explanations to my brother. "Governor Mason agreed to push our budget reform proposal through if Nico and I pretended to be dating in public. She wanted the people to get used to the idea of a human caring deeply about a vampire, so there wouldn't be as much uproar when the East End's school budget was slashed to make more money for the West End children, and much of the East End's public works budget was reallocated so the entire city was serviced fairly."

Declan snorts. "Isn't that just fantastic. Nico would never go for something like that."

I motion to my face. "Clearly."

Orlando stands straighter, as if needing to compensate since Declan witnessed his almost blush when I called him "my big sweetie pie". "Let's get going."

Though I don't know where he is leading me, I trust Orlando's instincts. If he needs me hidden while he deals with Nico, then I am not going to make a big fuss about it. All I want is a nap and my pajamas. Since I won't be getting the first of those things, I opt to change into fuzzy pink pajamas before we leave, so at least I can be comfortable while my face throbs.

We pick up my prescription on the way while the three of us drive in silence to the destination Orlando will not disclose aloud. He is driving his black sedan while Declan and I sit together in the back on the leather seats, trying to remain calm at my sudden change of address.

"You're not trembling," Declan remarks, pointing to my hand when Orlando pulls onto the freeway. "Normally you would be shaking after a day this eventful. Guess your medicine is doing its job."

Orlando meets my eyes in the rearview mirror, and in that instant, I know why it is that my body is healing itself in ways it never could before.

My breath hitches. "It's your blood, Orlando. Ever since I started drinking it every night, I am steadier on my feet."

Declan sits up straighter. "Are you serious? Your doctor needs this information, Coco. If that's true, that's incredible!"

I frown at my brother. "No one can know that we're mated. You two are in the mess, so you're in on the secret. But no one else knows this sort of thing is even possible. Not my doctor, not the sheriff. Not anyone."

Declan's face pulls. "Not even Rome?"

I bristle at the name I have made perfectly clear I do not want to hear. "Mister Valentino wanted out, so that's what he's gotten. He doesn't know a thing about it, and that's how it should be."

Declan shoots Orlando a look of pure worry. "I want to

know this sort of thing. You want to be top of the list when my sister is hurt? Fine. I want to be top of the list when she's having a medical epiphany."

Orlando nods once. "Fair. Though, I didn't know that was happening. I should have. Mated vampires live longer and tend to heal quicker, but all of that is hearsay. I've never actually met a mated couple. And we don't have healthcare, so that's not something we can say with documented confidence."

The trees thicken the longer we drive. It's been a while since I was surrounded on both sides by nature with no buildings in sight. Maybe I should be worried that Orlando turns off the freeway at an exit with no visible trace of civilization. Perhaps I should be concerned that he turns down an unmarked dirt road and pulls into what can only be described as a shack.

I trust Orlando, even if it means letting him hide me in an old, abandoned cabin in the woods.

"Wait," Orlando bids us, his voice heavy with gravity. "I know how we can fix this with the governor. I know how we can get her to push our proposal through." He swallows hard, his words coming out like molasses. "She wanted you to pretend to date a vampire. You can still do that."

I have no idea what he could possibly suggest. "She seemed pretty specific, Orlando. It can't just be any vampire; it has to be a Valentino. And I'll be damned if either of your cousins volunteer for the job now."

Orlando hangs his head, gripping the steering wheel like it's someone who has personally offended his family's name. "Nico and Rome aren't the only Valentino men."

Declan sucks in a quick gasp.

Orlando turns to face me. "I can do it. If our little lie can give the next generation a fighting chance with a proper education, then I can hold your hand and whatnot."

My face pulls, which hurts and is wholly offensive, so I'm glad the darkness hides my initial reaction. "You're a decade older than I am."

"I hardly think that would be the part of the scandal people will be focusing on." Orlando waves off the idea. "We don't have to. It's fine. Just a suggestion. No bad ideas in brainstorming, right?"

I swallow hard, considering his offer. It's not the worst idea. In fact, it might be the only idea left.

Declan shoots me a look of warning. "Coco, no. This isn't... You don't have to... We'll find another way."

I gnaw on my lower lip and close my one good eye that isn't already swollen shut. "Declan, get your phone out. You're going to need to post a picture of this."

Declan squinches his eyes shut and punches the seat between us. "You're not a prop! You're a person! Am I the only one who understands that?"

I reach over and squeeze my brother's wrist. "Yes, you are. And it's your job to remind me of that fact. But for now, this is what I need to do." I force half a smile. "It's fine. It's a good idea, actually. I like spending time with Orlando rather than fighting with Nico. He already lives with me. This will work."

Declan looks like he wants to tell me off, but he keeps his mouth shut as he jerks open the backdoor and switches seats with Orlando, who slides into the back beside me.

When Declan gets out his phone, Orlando nods. "Take the picture."

"Of what? There's like, two feet of space between you. That's not a relationship, and neither of you look happy." The overhead light illuminates Declan's correct assessment. Neither of us can look at each other.

I can do better than this. I can fight harder for the vampire children's education.

I scoot closer, tapping Orlando under his chin. "Lean in, like we're two magnets that can't pull away from each other."

"That's stupid." Orlando's lips purse at the notion. "That's not what it's like."

My fingers twist in my lap. "I'm trying here, Orlando. Pretend you care about me."

Orlando sighs heavily. "You know I care about you. I wouldn't have moved in if I didn't."

That's certainly news to me. "I thought you were doing it to protect the vampires. If I'm stolen, my blood is used to kill your people."

His upper lip curls as if I have farted in his face. "You really think I don't care about you? When I found you in that basement back when you were a teenager, it broke me. Who do you think made sure your house had top notch security? Who made you breakfast this morning? Maybe that's not love or a relationship, but it's caring. I care. I know how to do the caring thing."

I snigger as he fumbles through his blustering. "Okay, then close your eyes. I can sell anything, even this."

"Fine. I'm closing my eyes." He squinches them tight like he is gearing up to take a punch in the gut.

"Not like that. Not like you're about to walk into a horror movie. Close them like you're about to drift off to sleep."

Orlando relaxes his face while my brother watches on in dread. My big sweetie pie's words come out quiet and only for me. "Your necklace. The one that Rome gave you that has a tracker on it."

"Shh," I scold him. "Don't say his name to me."

Orlando softens. "The necklace my cousin gave you that you took off and put in that box of stuff to give back to him? I put it in your overnight bag. If anything should happen... If I can't reach you in time, you have to twist the thing and send the signal to him."

I shake my head slowly. "He wouldn't come. He left me."

Orlando's fingers trill slowly down my forearm. "He

would come for you. If you run into trouble and I can't get there in time, send the signal. Please, Coco."

My mouth firms. "I would sooner die."

I angle Orlando's chin downward until his forehead presses to mine. The bruised side of my face is concealed from the camera, showcasing only the right side as my lashes flutter shut. I feather my fingers across Orlando's cheek. Even though it's a show, my stomach tightens at being close enough to a man to smell his aftershave.

Orlando's breath catches, his mouth an inch from mine. He moves his hand to rest overtop mine, showing off his ring that all the Valentino men wear with their family's crest emblazoned in the gold.

This morning that ring tore up my face. It was on Nico's hand, granted, but the stalwart nature of the Valentino men runs like an electric current through their blood.

I am grateful Orlando is gentle with me.

My heart is confused and nervous. I shouldn't be this close to Orlando. "Take the stinking picture, Declan."

My brother snaps out of his disgust and takes several from different angles, directing the tilt of our chins so he can get the perfect shot. "I don't want Orlando's whole face. The ring is enough. That way when Rome comes back..."

I know what my brother is thinking. Orlando and Rome look similar enough that, with Orlando's face partially obscured and the lighting dim enough, people will assume it is Rome in the backseat, making out with the Last Deadblood.

I should correct Declan, but I don't. Mostly because it doesn't matter at this point. It's all fake. If I am supposedly dating Orlando or Rome, it doesn't matter; neither scenarios are real.

Declan examines his phone. "Well, aren't I quite the photographer? I almost believe you two are in love, looking at a few of these."

Orlando and I pull away from each other, clearing our throats and trying to iron out the pink in our cheeks. "Great. Send it to all the news channels, post it on social media. Do everything to put that picture in front of people. I am not posing for another one until it's absolutely necessary," Orlando rules before he throws himself out of the car and stomps toward the rickety old cabin.

Declan helps me out of the car, shielding me from the wintry breeze. He lets me lean on him as we walk to the dilapidated front door. "Are you ready for this?" my brother asks me in a hushed voice, as if not wanting to wake the woods from their moonlit slumber.

Of course I'm not ready. No one is ever prepared to go into hiding, however dire the situation grows. But I place one foot in front of the other, forcing myself to accept that my life is about to take another unexpected turn.

I can only hope we survive all that Mayfield has broken

in us, so the city we have fought for does not destroy us completely.

Love the book?
Leave a review!
Otherwise, Rome dies.

29

THE FORBIDDEN CITY PREVIEW

Enjoy a Free Preview of *The Forbidden City*, Book Four in the Last Deadblood Series

My Dearest Love

I didn't pack a brush. In my haste to get somewhere safe, I didn't remember to pack a hairbrush. I guess I was more focused on escaping the city after Nico—my childhood best friend—publicly spat on me, then kicked and punched my face until it was black and blue.

At least I have a toothbrush, so there's that silver lining.

Actually, Orlando did the packing for me, but I try not to blame him for anything that was forgotten. He got me safely out of Mayfield, which was the right call.

Of all the twists and turns I anticipated when I moved back to Mayfield, intent on opening up a business that served both vampires and humans in Midtown, ending up in this rickety old cabin in the middle of the woods outside the city proper wasn't in the plan. Though I don't disagree with Orlando's insistence that I relocate here temporarily until Nino-Bear can be sorted out, this whole situation is less than ideal.

Not Nino-Bear. Nico. Nico Valentino is the man who beat me up. Nino-Bear is the mischievous boy I used to make mud pies with, back when life was simple and loving people was easy.

Nino-Bear doesn't exist anymore.

What a coincidence; neither does the girl in pigtails who used to make him laugh when he grew afraid of the big men with guns.

Though, as he is now one of the big men with guns, I imagine he has fewer things of which to be afraid.

Not me. I have plenty to fear, not the least of which are the spiders in this pre-war cabin in the middle of nowhere. Certainly this is a place a girl goes to be murdered and never heard from again. My cell phone doesn't have reception, though perhaps this is a good thing. I don't want to hear what the people of Mayfield are saying.

I'm sure the lie of me taking up with a vampire is well circulated by now.

It wouldn't have been a lie two months ago, yet here we are.

I wanted to be my mother—to pick up her mantle of being a vampire rights activist and lead the way for not just tolerance but acceptance of those different than us. She met with dignitaries and important policymakers, weighing in on issues with the gravity of someone who had been elected as a public servant.

Funny that nature selected her to be a weapon.

She was the Last Deadblood until she had me, and now I am the final weapon. My blood can be used to kill vampires, who generally live far sturdier lives than humans. But I don't want to be a beacon for war. I love the Valentino family—the head family of the vampire people. Or at least I used to.

Now I'm not so sure.

Nico was supposed to pretend to be my boyfriend. It was a dreadful plan, to be sure, but when Governor Ingrid Mason stops by, you go along with whatever she says. What I wanted was for the education budget to be divided equally in Mayfield, so that the vampire children in the West End had the same quality of books, computers and education as the privileged human East End children. What I wanted was for the city's public works budget to be split evenly, as well. That shouldn't be so hard a feat to accomplish, but apparently, I picked a stubborn issue for my first one to tackle.

I wanted to be like my mother and affect change with an effortless smile so the world wouldn't be so grim.

I didn't realize how much effort goes into concocting an effortless smile.

It was an uphill battle with no hope of success until Governor Mason promised to throw her weight behind the proposal if I did one thing.

I needed to pretend to be dating a member of the Valentino family.

If only she knew the head of the Valentinos had recently broken my heart and ran off with the thing. Had she asked a month earlier, I would have proudly come out as dating the handsomest, noblest and most accomplished man I'd ever known.

Unfortunately, Mister Valentino turned out to be nothing short of ordinary. The moment things got too real for him, he split, ending what I thought was love without so much as a conversation.

It's just as well. I don't have time for silly things like love. I have history to change and minds to open. A pretend boyfriend is far better for the sort of life I lead.

I didn't expect it would be Orlando—the Valentino cousin who acts as their sentry.

I also didn't mean to mate with him. Though, to be fair, little is known about the vampiric mating bond. We're still learning the ropes as we go. For example, we learned that if I drink a little of Orlando's blood before bed in my evening tea, ailments that have taken a toll on my body for years seem to vanish. But if I miss a night, I am so cold by morning that not even the hottest bath can warm my skin.

Orlando gave me a flask of his blood to keep at the cabin while he's away dealing with Nico. He is also juggling the mess Mister Valentino left him in the West End when he split so abruptly. I'm to splash a few drops of Orlando's blood into my tea at night, giving Orlando a longer tether so he doesn't have to come back here every evening and risk leading a tail to the cabin who might want to abduct me.

It's laughable that anyone might believe the man a decade my senior, this family friend, might be the man I end up with. But for the sake of getting the education budget revisions passed sooner than next fall, I pray the world believes the staged photo of Orlando and I getting cozy in the backseat of his car is real.

I was in love with Orlando's cousin, but only Orlando, my brother, and his boyfriend know that.

My blood could kill Orlando. Still, the mirage of me dating a Valentino is what the governor requires, so that is the show we have given her.

Declan positioned the photo so Orlando's face was obscured by our hands, leaving it uncertain which Valentino I am dating, since Rome and Orlando look so similar. But the gold ring all the Valentino men wear with the family crest was visible, so the people have all the ingredients needed to make a rumor truly grow wings and fly.

I am far removed from the internet or any living thing (other than the spiders), so I have no idea if anyone bought the lie or not.

Either way, I decide to occupy my time this evening scribbling in a notebook Orlando brought me.

He does that sometimes—brings me something I desperately long to have but never asked for. It's part of the mate bond. He knows me well, even if he doesn't mean to be paying attention.

I wanted a journal to keep myself company while I remain isolated, so the next day, he showed up with groceries, a few changes of clothes and a journal, even though I never mentioned I wanted one.

It's silly, really. And Orlando is the opposite of silly. But my pen drags across the unlined beige pages, writing a letter to Orlando to make him laugh, and also to share my madness with someone.

I start out the letter in grand fashion, pretending we are soulmates separated by fate's cruel hand. In my lonely life overseas before moving back to Mayfield, I dreamed of having a dearest love to whom I could write sappy sonnets.

Orlando will tolerate my goofiness.

. . .

'MY DEAREST LOVE,

I PINE FOR YOU DAILY, AS IS MY RITUAL. EVERYTHING REMINDS me of you. For instance, a spider landed on my toothbrush this morning. I missed you so badly that I plucked off six of his legs and paraded him around, pretending he was you. I was so good at conjuring your likeness in my imagination that I only remembered the spider was not you when I was kissing the hairy pest, and he up and died in lieu of returning my affections.

How I pine for your songs.

I SNICKER AT THE IDEA OF ORLANDO SINGING AT ALL. I CAN barely believe I've seen him smile.

WHEN YOU SING OF MY BEAUTY, IT MAKES MY BREASTS GROW three sizes. They rise to your song like unrequited mountains. Sing to me, my love. For without your melody, I fear my melons might shrivel up to mere raisins, and my soul shall in turn wither. For you are the sun, the stars and the entire solar system, while I am but a helpless, demure flower.

Pluck me, my dearest love. My big sweetie pie.

-COLETTE

. . .

I READ IT AGAIN, LAUGHING AT MY PROSE. I PLAN ON READING this to Orlando in grand fashion in a lilting voice with plenty of theatrics.

If he ever comes back here. If he doesn't, I might die in the woods without anyone knowing where I've gone.

No, no. I shake that thought away because it simply isn't true. Declan knows where I am. He won't let me disappear, and neither will Orlando.

I haven't seen anyone in four days, though. Orlando brought me more than enough food to last the week, but after that...

I'm sure he'll come back any minute now.

Any minute now.

Continue the series with *The Forbidden City* today!